The Burgess Theory

Tobi Nifesi

DEDICATION

To my dad, Lawrence Olunifesi

See you in heaven, sometime.

DISCLAIMER

The names of characters and details of stories shared in this book are entirely fictional and were not written in reference to any real-life experiences.

That being said, there are a few nameless characters in this book.

Tobi Nifesi

PART ONE

Tobi Nifesi

PROLOGUE

February 15, 2017

The blond waitress stepped back into the room. This time, she carried a bowl of rice with mini-shrimp rolls dipped in it and made her way to the corner of the room where they stood.

"She's coming back." Kim smiled at her husband, and hovered her glass of wine over her mouth, "I bet you $20 that she's going to circle back this way first."

"You're onto her, aren't you?" He laughed but never took his eyes off Kim and her wrap skirt midi dress.

His bride, of three years, rarely ever stepped out for these sorts of events but tonight, she had done so in such ravishing style. He held his hand around her neck and gently fondled with the hook-and-eye closure at the back of her satin dress; making sure not to untie her as he did.

"Are you game or what?" Kim shot a glance at him, "She's going to come here first and I'm going to prove you wrong."

"I don't need you to prove me wrong, I know you're wrong, honey. She's just making her regular rounds and she's probably just used to a particular route."

"Yeah? A route that just happens to start with you?"

He laughed again.

"Alright," He said, and finally considered Kim's theory that the blond waitress had a crush on him and was deliberately serving him first whenever she made her way around the room with small bites. "I'm game but we have to up the stakes."

"Oh?" Kim's face lit up, "$500 then?"

"No, not money. That's too easy. Plus, you would never pay up."

Kim chuckled, "But I would. I absolutely would."

"Honey, we both know you wouldn't. Not falling for that. If we are going to do this, it has to be a solid bet. Something you don't like for something I don't like."

"What do you have in mind?"

"You're not going to like it." He gave his best impression of a hellish smile and stared at her until she understood.

"No." Kim gasped, "No, no, no, not that. I'm not doing that."

"You'll only have to do it if you lose. If you're so confident that you're right about this then you don't have anything to worry about."

Kim remained silent for a moment and turned her attention towards the waitress who was still making her way across the room. Her husband had bet on one of her major pet peeves and she knew that if he won this bet, not only will she have to hold her end of the deal, but she wouldn't hear the last of it.

"Do we have a deal?" He asked,

She was going to say no and counter with a bet that she could at least live with but then she realized the waitress hadn't broken her stride yet and wasn't so far off anymore.

"And if I win, what would you have to do?" She shot back, with a sly grin on her face.

"You tell me."

"We'll get a cat." The words fell right off her lips like she had been urging to say it for a long time.

"No, no, we are not doing that."

"That's a strong wager," She said, "For what you want me to do, that's a pretty strong match."

He threw his hands in the air, albeit gently, "How is that a match? You would only have to do it once, but I would have to live with the cat for the rest of its life."

"Who says I'd only do it once?" She bit the side of her pink lower lip and felt his chest with her right palm.

"You're serious?"

"Yeah, I am."

"You can't be." He rolled his eyes at her, "There's no way. I've been asking you for this for three years. We've spoken about it and you're just going to change your mind over some random waitress?"

"Let's just say I'm feeling confident. This or my cat. Let the best Grant win." She said, referencing their surname.

Together, they turned their attention towards the waitress and did their best to be inconspicuous about their little game. Kim could feel her stomach turn. Maybe this was a bad idea. Maybe their wager didn't need to have anything at stake. It was supposed to be just a fun way to distract themselves instead of interacting with other couples at the event. They might have just taken it too far.

Despite her doubts, she didn't call it off. She had seen things like this before and a part of her knew she was right. Women eyed her husband every time they went out together. From the air hostess on their flights to the server across the bar in their favorite local coffee shop, some young woman was always checking her husband out. She would point it out to him but he would dismiss it with comments like "You need to stop worrying about what other eyes are doing, focus on mine." or "You're the only psychotherapist here. No one else is using their eyes to analyze others."

She would ignore him.

It made perfect sense to her. Her husband's height, defined cheekbones and lush gold hair made him easy on the eyes. Who could resist staring at that? She would stare too if she wasn't already with him. It was happening again tonight. The waitress had been staring and acting all too cordial to not be an admirer. He couldn't see it but she did, and she was about to prove him wrong again.

Kim was so certain she was about to win the wager but much to her dismay, the blond waitress came close to where they stood, sidestepped them and walked away towards a couple standing by the windows that lined the east wall of the room.

He burst out laughing, uncontrollably.

Two hours later, Kim stood – with her left elbow planted over the back of her right hand – and stared at her reflection in the bathroom mirror. She shook her head at the thought of what she was about to do. All through her adult life, she'd sworn she would never do this with a man. She was a firm believer that such acts were just as condescending to women as they were skanky. It was one of the first things she'd discussed with her husband as they made wedding plans together, three years ago. She had been very forthright about it and that took him by surprise.

"Really?" He'd asked, with a mildly confused look, "Bad experience? Or that's just a personal preference?"

"It's demeaning to women." She replied, "There's nothing satisfying about it."

"Satisfying for whom?"

"I don't know," Kim shrugged, "What's the point of it? It's just… I don't know. It's nasty."

He'd laid his back on a couch across from her but sat up to give her a stern look.

"Now I want to know what happened," He said, "Something must have happened to you."

"What do you mean?"

"What do you mean what do I mean? I'm guessing you feel this way because something happened while you were doing it right? Did you swallow or something?"

Kim threw a pillow at him from the sofa where she sat. He dodged it and broke into a series of chuckles. She was being teased and that was always his go-to whenever she had her serious face on – yet she really wanted him to hear what she had to say and not belittle the moment.

She really meant this.

"I don't swallow, you know that. I'd never put myself in that kind of situation. I just don't like it and we won't be doing any of that."

"Hold on, hold on, hold on," He rose to his feet

and strode towards her until he got close enough to sit beside her, he said, "That's a decision we have to make together, isn't it?"

"I don't think so." She shrugged, "It's my choice and I'm choosing not to do that."

"Really?" He asked, "What if I told you I like it?"

"I don't know, we'd have to figure something out. There are many other things we can do, but I'm not doing that."

"We'd have to talk about this later."

"But," She started, "We are already talking about it right now."

"I don't think we should." He held his arms around her now and made her rest her head on his chest, "We have to find a compromise. Come to some sort of…"

"Is this your way of telling me you like it?" She shot back at him, "cause if it is, you should definitely reconsider all of this."

He liked it but never reconsidered his choice to take her as his bride. Yet, three years later, he was about to get what he wanted. Kim straightened her bra and tucked her left breast in until it was firmly behind the tricot undergarment. Through her reflection in the mirror, she could see that her braided bun wasn't as firm as it ought to be so, with both hands, she packed her brown hair and gathered it all back into its pleat.

Kim was draped in nothing, but a brassiere and a thong roped around her pelvis. After taking one more look at herself, she turned around, made her way out of the bathroom and into their bedroom where he laid on his back against the headboard. His eyes followed her as she walked around the corner of the bed and slipped the lower half of her body underneath the duvet.

The grin on his face said it all. He'd won the wager and was about to reap his reward: for the very first time, his wife was about to perform fellatio on him. Nothing else made sense at that moment.

The hair on his back stood and the neurons in his head went flying helter-skelter as she traced a path from his chest to the single button on his loose underpants using the fingers on her left hand. Eventually, she found the bulge and gripped it – it got even stiffer as she held it and then began stroking it.

He turned and met her gaze. She had a slight smirk on her face as if to say, she was in control now – and by all means, she was. He tried to edge closer to her to unhook her bra, but she shook her head to stop him and when he tried to speak, she whispered, "shhh."

Then, it began. She slid down slowly until she was fully underneath the duvet and found her way to the division between his legs. As soon as she found her balance, she pulled down his underpants but made sure his shaft was out of the way. Her eyes were shut but her mouth knew where to go. Upon first contact, she let out a quick and involuntary sigh. It got easier after that. First, she licked it a couple times and then, took it in. She moved her mouth up and down, finding her rhythm as she did.

Not too long after that, he gripped the bedsheets and pulled at it. When he could no longer hold back his urges, he pulled the duvet off her back, and that brought her rhythm to a pause. Then, he grabbed her by the waist and gently turned her around until she laid with her back against the bed. She reached for her thong, but he got there faster than she could and helped her out of it. She returned the favour by using her hand to slip him inside her.

Once she had him deep inside, he began thrusting back and forth. Slowly enough for her to feel him but sudden enough for him to go deeper with each thrust. He knew he was there when she began moaning. It went on for a while and then her moaning turned into sharp whimpers. At first, he didn't think much of it, but the whimpers got louder. He stopped to take a good look at her and was stunned to see her eyes soaked with tears.

"What's wrong?" He pulled out immediately, "Are you okay?"

Kim turned around, dipped her face in her palms and began crying. He held her and tried to turn her face towards him, but she wouldn't move.

"Why are you crying?" He was getting increasingly panicky, "Did I do something wrong?"

Still weeping, she shook her head.

Just then, he saw it. There was blood on their bedsheets right around the corner where her bottom had been planted just a minute ago.

"You're bleeding!"

"I know," She said with a muffled voice, "It hurts!"

"Why? Did I do something? Are you on your period? Are you? Why didn't you say something? What do you need me to get you? What can I do?"

"Stop! Just stop it." Kim rose from the bed and got off it then began walking towards the bedroom. "Just stop."

He went after her and caught her in her stride just before she could open the bathroom door.

"What is going on?" He held her head against his chest, tried to calm her down and asked again, "Are you okay? Talk to me."

"It's not you," She managed to say, "It's just a bad

spot. You hit a spot that you shouldn't have."

ONE

May 12, 2017

It was as shiny as they get and the cut around its edges made it stand out amongst the cluster of diamonds. Yet, Chris knew this wasn't the one. Granted, he had no idea what the right one was but he knew he would know when he saw it.

For now, he wandered around the diamond store and peered into cases and glass boxes over and over. This was his third time, in the past two weeks, in the store. Today, he had to make a choice. Even Amina, the store owner couldn't help him today. She's given him all the education he needed and now, he just had to apply it and make a concrete decision.

There were so many of them to choose from but with Amina's help, he's been able to narrow it down to a few selections. She told him all about the four Cs of diamonds. The Cs – Color, Clarity, Cut and Carat Weight – are the universal standard for categorizing diamonds. They help both buyers and sellers to communicate in a clear language when describing diamonds.

When deciding on a diamond to buy, a buyer has to first consider its color – colorless or light – and its clarity – the nature of its inclusions and blemishes. Once a decision is made on the diamond's color and clarity, the buyer would go on to choose their choice of cut – how the diamond divide the light that bounces off it – and finally the carat – the weight of the diamond.

For a young man in his mid-twenties, whose presumptive knowledge of diamonds was limited to the two rings left behind by his parents, Chris had been overwhelmed by the depth of information surrounding diamonds. Although he was a homeowner and an investor, he had never had to purchase an item so complicated and fiddly.

Two weeks ago, after Amina had narrated a good deal about the four Cs, he sunk into the chair in her office across the table from her and said, "I just want a ring."

"I know and this is how you make a choice." Amina tilted her head slightly to the left, causing her loosely unpacked braids to fall gently on her shoulders, "All we have to do is make a selection in these four categories. Better yet, if you know what she likes, that might make things a lot easier for you."

"Pssh…" Chris shrugged, "How would I know what choice of ring she likes. She's never been engaged, and no one randomly talks about their choice of rings.

You know what I mean?"

"Does she wear any kind of rings as part of her accessories?"

He thought about it for a second, then replied, "Yeah, I think so. I think she does."

"What do they look like? Do you know? Or do you have an idea what her ring size is? Maybe we could start there?"

Chris could tell that Amina was getting somewhere with her questions, but he knew it was going to be futile anyway, because he didn't have the answers.

"To be honest with you," Chris shook his head, "I have no idea. I know people have different ring sizes, but I never even knew there was a metric for it. I'm not sure I can make a decision today. Not until I think deeply about the four Cs, at the very least. You know what I mean?"

Amina nodded, "I understand. In that case, I will give you this brochure. It has the necessary information that can guide you as you think about it. Also, here's my business card. If you have any question, you can give me a call or send me an email."

"Thank you." Chris collected the brochure and business card from Amina.

"You should probably talk to her too," Amina said as Chris was about stepping out of her office. "In no certain terms, just see where she's at with all this."

Chris turned around just in time to see Amina's face before she finished her last sentence. Her head was tilted to the right this time, her eyes tight and worried. He wasn't quite sure if it was a sales tactic for her to act emotionally invested in her client's decision-making process or if she was genuinely concerned about him.

"With all of what? A proposal or the ring?" Chris

asked, without stepping away from the door.

"Both." Amina replied, "You seem like a nice young man and I thought I should just point that out. You're about to make a very expensive purchase so I think it's only right for me to help you get this right."

"Thank you," Chris wasn't sure what to say, "I appreciate your concern, but I'll figure it out. If I have any questions, I'll let you know."

That was two weeks ago. At the moment, he was sure about one thing: he was looking for a colorless (D) internally flawless three-carat diamond with an excellent cut. All he had to do was decide on the brand and Amina would be sending him off once and for all.

Chris stood over the glass box and peered through it at one of the Noam Carver Engagement rings. Amina walked over to where he stood but didn't say a word until he did.

"I promise you I'm going to make a choice today." Chris started, "I have a deadline to meet and it's almost here. I have to do this by next week."

"Good to see you again, Chris." Amina said, ignoring Chris' remarks, "Don't worry, this is only your third time here. We've had men come in here every week for months and still couldn't decide on what they want."

They both giggled.

Chris added, "It almost seems like men are decisive until they have to pick engagement rings."

"Well," Amina inserted her key into the keyhole in the glass box before them and reached for one of the rings, "You can't blame them. People consider the choice of an engagement ring – much like the choice of a husband or wife – to be a once in a lifetime decision. People try to be careful not to make the wrong choice. I take it this is the one you're looking at. The solitaire? Right?"

He nodded

Amina held the ring with a three-carat center in her palm and stretched her hand towards Chris so he could have a better look at the tiny object.

"Would you like me to put it under a 'scope for you?" Amina asked,

"You mean a Microscope?"

"Yeah, there's one in my office. If you want to have a clearer look at the ring, that would make it a lot easier."

"Sure, why not?"

The walk to Amina's office took seconds and soon they were sitting across each other just like they did two weeks ago when she taught him all he needed to know about diamonds. She placed the ring on the microscope slide and fastened it with the stage clips. Then, she turned the coarse focus knob to move the objective lens closer to the slide. When she was done, she gestured at Chris to have a look.

"It's beautiful," Chris muttered, with his eyes set over the eyepiece. "and bright too."

"You might want to adjust the illuminator to reduce the amount of light getting on the slide," Amina suggested, then she adjusted it for him anyway.

"Oh yeah, it's a lot clearer now," Chris remarked.

"I take it you spoke with her?" Amina didn't wait for Chris to lift his eyes from the eyepiece before she started quizzing him, "…about everything?"

"Uhm," Chris moved away from the microscope and glanced at her, "Yeah, kind of. It's supposed to be a surprise so I had to be careful not to get into details, but I know her ring size and I'm pretty sure I have a good idea about the kind of rings she would like."

"How did you find that out?"

"I found one of her rings and I measured the size. That's how I found out the ring size. Last week, we were at a hotel, having breakfast and I made a comment about the ring on the finger of a woman who was sitting with her partner at the table adjacent to ours. One thing led to another and we ended up talking about ring preferences at a very high level. That helped me put two and two together. You know what I mean?"

"Sure," Amina said, "I'm sure she would like it. How long have you guys been together?"

"A year."

Amina tried to hide the look of shock on her face, but Chris caught it.

"Yeah, I know what you're thinking." Chris started, "It's a short time to start thinking about engagement. I was thinking that too, but you know what? When you know, you know. She's perfect, you know what I mean? She's everything you need in a companion. We complete each other in every way."

"That's good for you." Amina smiled at him, "That's really what everyone should say about their ideal partner. If she makes you feel that way, then she's a keeper. I'm happy for you. Do you feel comfortable with this choice?"

"With her or the ring?"

"Oh, the ring. I'm talking about the ring. Do you want to go ahead and pay for that?"

"Yeah, yeah. This is the one." Chris grinned from ear to ear, "I told you I was going to decide today."

Amina pulled the microscope closer to herself, adjusted the objective lens until the microscope slide was far enough from it. She took the ring off the microscope and placed it on a miniature pillow in a box. Then, she walked out of the room with the box in hand. A few minutes later, she came back in with brown box in one hand and payment machine in the other.

"Here you go," She placed the box in a small branded plastic bag, and set the payment machine in front of Chris – close enough for him to reach it, "How would you like to pay for this? Would you like to pay 10% deposit now or…?"

"No, no, no." Chris immediately rebuffed her suggestion, "I'm good for it. I'll pay at once."

"Oh, sure." Amina did her best not to sound surprised. Clearly, she had underestimated her client's financial status. She'd thought one of the reasons he couldn't come to a conclusion on what ring to buy was because he was working with a tight budget but now, she knew she might have been wrong.

Within minutes, Chris paid for the ring and was on his way out. Amina walked him to the store entrance and as they shook hands, she said, "Thank you and congratulations to you and… what was her name?"

"Beth," Chris replied, "Her name is Beth."

"Right, Beth. Congratulations to you and Beth."

They parted ways. Amina walked back to her office, shut the door behind her and grabbed her iPhone from one of the pockets in the pintuck track pants she had on. She dialed a number and waited for the ringer to go on and then off.

"Hey, he just left." Amina started, then paused for the person on the receiving end of the call to respond, "Yes, he did. He bought the ring and he's going to be proposing next week. The last time he was here, he said he was taking her away for a weekend in Minnesota and was going to propose. So, he's probably travelling there soon."

She paused again, and when the person she had called was done speaking, she said, "Beth. He said her name is Beth."

TWO

May 20, 2017

I don't want to talk about her. Come on, don't make me do that. We are here, she's not. What does it matter? You know what I mean?

What? What was that? How did I meet her? Come on, why does it matter? Okay, you know what? If I tell you, would you let this go? Cause, to be honest, I don't think we need to go into all those details. Clearly, you're cool with this so everything else shouldn't matter, you know what I mean?

Sure, sure.

At the time, I had just started my investment firm. Before that, I was working with a hedge fund as a portfolio manager. Our clients were my responsibility. I had to make sure I got all the necessary information from them and presented the hedge fund's discretionary investment offerings in a clear and appealing manner. After that, I would develop proposals based on their needs. It was that kind of work – very direct and in-your-face – but that also meant I had to be as sociable as possible.

I had to develop essential relationships with potential clients and help them get to a point where they could trust me. For the most part, I think I did a really good job with that.

You know why I say so? What ended up happening is that these potential clients – in fact, even existing ones – began walking up to me and giving me totally off-the-record information. Based on the positive relationship I had with them, I would also share off-the-record market and investment strategies with them. It didn't take too long before I realized what was going on. I had made a name for myself in the industry and I was a brand of my own. I was working for a hedge fund, but my reputation was beginning to be more trustworthy than that of the hedge fund I work with – and I was a mere portfolio manager.

Can you imagine that? I wasn't an executive or anything like that, but I pulled more weights than those on the top floor.

When I realized that, I knew it was time to step away. I resigned and spoke to a few guys I knew on Bay Street – you know, Canada's version of Wall Street – just to see who might be interested in teaming up to start an investment firm that is solely about the clients. I wanted to start something that prioritizes the client first. That was my goal. It took a while and eventually this dude, who I had once worked with while on an assignment in Toronto, reached out to me. Michael

Baumgartner is his name. He gave me a call one Saturday morning and he went on and on about how frustrated he was with the hedge fund he worked with out there. He talked my ear off that day, but I listened because I understood how he felt. We shared similar frustrations. Before the end of the call, I told him to fly down to my city…

What? Where do I live? What does it matter? I don't think it matters. Come on, I'm telling you a good story. You asked for it so just let me get through it. You know what I mean?

Anyway, Michael flew out the next weekend and we met at the restaurant in the hotel he was staying at. We talked for hours and hours and when I was sure that I had properly sized him up, I told him about my idea to start a new investment firm. Before I was done talking, he was sold on it. It was just perfect. It was like I was talking to my reflection. He had similar ideas and we were perfectly on the same page. Right there, we drafted a rough plan and set out to start the firm.

Within a couple of months, we had rented out a room in a coworking space downtown and had started making calls. It was a bunch of really annoying cold calls at first but few weeks after, we booked our first gig and it was like the floodgates opened up right after that. So, here I was – a 25-year-old black man making a very decent paycheck with no clue how to spend it. I decided to do something my folks – bless their souls – taught me to do whenever I got money.

Guess what that is?

Did you say tithe?

No, it's not that but it's pretty close. My parents were not really big on churches, but I guess they had a similar mentality to what tithes are supposed to be like.

Anyway, when I was younger, they had started this foundation for orphans back home – you know, like where I'm originally from.

What? No, no, no. Again, listen that little bit of detail doesn't matter. Let me get through the story. I'm almost done I promise.

My parents had this foundation or orphanage – however you want to call it – and they made us – you know, my sister and me – donate at least 10% of our allowance to the orphanage every month. I mean, I guess it was a noble thing to teach an eight-year-old. It stuck with me anyway and so, even at age 25, it was the first thing I could think of when figuring out how to spend my money.

I found out about this non-profit in my city that helped child cancer patients get the treatments they need, and I was drawn to all that they stood for as an organization – their mandate, initiative, everything. I decided to start making occasional anonymous donations to that non-profit. The plan was to leave no traces of course but I messed up with my second donation and I think they could tell my contact information from my wire transfer.

I knew it was only a matter of time before they reached out to me and surely enough, they did. They rang my cell and when I picked up the call, I was greeted by the most angelic voice I had ever heard. It was so soft and soothing – like sweet nothing.

You know that song, yeah?

Right, just like that. She suggested we schedule a meeting via video call to discuss further and you know, I fancied the idea of putting a face to the voice and what not so we scheduled it and when we eventually had the meeting, it was one of the most amazing experiences of my life.

She had this long, I don't know what you would call it, kind of like kohl-black hair that flowed over her shoulders and was a sharp contrast to her pale glossy-looking skin. She was divine, I tell you. As she spoke, all I could do was stare at her halo-white teeth. Her words were eloquent and brimmed with confidence. I tried to keep the conversation brief and professional but as soon as I got off that call, I knew I had to speak with her again somehow.

Wait? Isn't this weird for you? Why would you want me to speak about someone else this way?

Does this turn you on?

No?

So, what's the point?

Alright, if you say so.

Anyway, I took the cheeky route of sending flowers to her office with a card.

What did the card say?

Uhm, I think it was something like:

When next can I see that smile? Tuesday, 7 pm, The Palms Lounge maybe?

I don't know, something like that. It worked anyway and that was it. We met at the Palms. It was as pretty as a picture and she looked even more beddable in person.

Anyway, long story short. We started dating and got married about two years ago.

What went wrong? I don't know. She lost her spark, I guess. There's this aura that she had when we first got together. She was bold, confident, walked with her head held high and I liked that about her, but I feel like as we got to know each other especially as a married couple, she just began to seem weak. I couldn't recognize the woman I had met at the Palms Lounge anymore. It's like one day I woke up and all her wits, charm and comeliness had been thrown out the window. I tried to get with the new program but at some point, I just couldn't stand her anymore.

I only stayed with her this long because she's an easy lay, you know what I mean? A guy like me – with my reputation as someone with a very shrewd business acumen – it is safer and much more respectable for me to have a woman at home. It speaks volume about my professionalism. To be very honest with you, that is why she still carries my last name. She means nothing to me.

I know how that sounds but in the spirit of transparency, like you asked for, that's the truth about how I got here. Don't get me wrong, she's an amazing person but getting married to her was a big mistake. I shouldn't have gotten married to her when I did, maybe I should've taken my time to really get to know her and see different facets of her personality. All of this would've been avoided, you know what I mean?

There were times when I thought I was wrong for feeling this way or falling out of love with her, but I don't think so anymore. If I truly love someone, I should be able to accommodate everything about them – their good and bad. I should be willing to compromise. I've tried that but it's not working. I can't deal with her bad days and I can't bring myself to deal with some of her weaknesses either. Instead, it just makes me really frustrated and mad at her. You know what I mean?

Do I feel what?

Do I feel like I'm misdirecting my anger?

Uhm, I don't know. Can you rephrase your question?

Am I projecting my personal frustrations on her? That's a good question actually. I don't know, maybe I am. I'm usually pretty good at making good decisions – as an investor and a person who engages people in a decision-making process. I guess I always thought that as a good judge of character, I would make the right choice when the time came to get married, but I was wrong. I made the wrong choice and I know I have to deal with that but it's stupidly frustrating because every day, she reminds me of the one time I really messed up.

You've been hoarding that blunt too long. Can I get a whiff of that?

Thank you.

What about you? Are you married?

It doesn't have to be all about me. I've shared a good deal, it's your turn.

You don't have a ring on, so I take it you're single, yeah?

Oh, come on, that's not fair. You've got to give me something to work with here.

Alright, I'm listening.

THREE

February 15, 2017

Her face was drenched with tears – the drops rolled down her cheeks, off her skin and formed a small pool of liquid on the vessel sink in the bathroom. The pain was wearing off, but the shame lingered long enough to bring back the memories of a night she thought she had long forgotten.

Shame has a way of doing that to you – it smears your canvas of positivity with thoughts of guilt, inadequacies and regret. Sometimes, these thoughts are founded in real-life situations or experiences that we wish we could just forget forever. Shame brings it all back and forces you to replay it in your head, over and over again, until you believe that you are defined by those experiences.

Kim knew this. As a psychotherapist, she had helped several patients work through this, so she knew how difficult it is to deal with a self-conscious emotion like shame. She reached for the paper towel that hung on the holder to the right of the vessel sink. She wiped her tears and washed her face. Her husband's voice grew louder – she had previously, subconsciously, turned down his volume – but now she let herself hear him clearly from where he stood behind the locked bathroom door.

"Are you okay?" "Do you need anything?" "Honey, talk to me." "What is going on?" "I'm going to bring down this door if you don't say something." "Just say something, anything." "Kim, Kim." "Kim, can you hear me?" "Should I call your mom?"

He's been going on and on, repeating these words but she tuned it all out until now. Kim knew she had to tell him something to alleviate his fears. She had two options: tell him all about that night or just come up with a simple believable story. She was good at the latter – she's heard all sorts of stories from her patients that she could easily insert herself into one of them and give a very plausible excuse to get out of any situation.

This had come in handy a few times – one of those moments occurred recently when she was pulled over by a cop. Mindlessly, she had been doing an 80 on a 50 trying to make it in time for a meeting. The deafening sound of the siren brought her back to her senses and shortly after, she had to park her Toyota Venza by the roadside and engage in a tête-à-tête with a uniform.

When she realized that the conversation wasn't going in her favour and she was about to get a hefty fine, she resorted to lying using one of her patient's true stories.

"I know it's not an excuse," She said, making all sorts of clueless and anxious facial expressions, "but my dad's on his death bed and I really have to get to him before he goes away. I'm sorry I wasn't thinking. My mind is everywhere and nowhere. I'm a mess, I know and I'm sorry. I just don't know what to do…"

Then, she bowed her head and began to breathe uncontrollably as though she were crying. At first, the man in the uniform didn't budge. Instead, he went on a tirade about how she could have been heading for her own death if he hadn't stopped her. Kim didn't break the act. She went on with her silent sobs and heavy breathing. Before she knew it, the cop handed her a handkerchief, told her to stop crying and suggested that he gave her ride instead of her driving in her condition.

She shook her head, slowly, and declined. He insisted but she suggested he drove behind her until she arrived at her destination. He obliged and refrained from ticketing her. She drove a few meters down to a hospital not far from where she had been stopped. Once they arrived, she went into the hospital and waited till she could see the cop drive away into the distance. As soon as the coast was clear, she got back into her vehicle and resumed speeding to catch with up with her meeting.

Telling a believable story had saved her on that day and now, she contemplated telling her husband something just as silly and likely – something about women that he probably couldn't understand or question. She could do that today but deep down, she knew she couldn't keep hiding this part of herself. What happened actually happened and she can't deny that, but she wished it didn't have such a lasting effect on her.

"Kim, I'm going to bring down this door." Her husband repeated, "I'm trying to respect your wish to be alone, but you've been in there for almost an hour. It makes no sense. I just want to know if you are okay or if there's something we need to do."

Kim closed her eyes – she didn't have much time. She had to decide how to handle the situation. Her husband wasn't your typical dude. He wore his heart on his sleeve and was quick to express his feelings. The downside of that is that he couldn't stomach the truth sometimes. Knowing that, she had to be careful not to get him overly worried or anxious. Yet, as she stood there in that bathroom contemplating what to say to him, she was feeding his anxiety.

"Kim, I'm coming in. Is that okay?"

She took a deep breath, straightened the nightgown she had put on when she walked into the bathroom and turned towards the door. The door opened as she was about to turn the knob. He stood there staring at her – she stared back at him.

"I'm okay," She said, with a faint voice, "I'm okay."

"What's going on?" He reached for her hands and pulled her closer to him, "What happened?"

"Let's sit down and talk about it." She replied, "I have something to tell you."

"Okay, sure."

Together, they walked over to their bed; she sat at the corner of the bed, but he pulled the sofa in their room closer towards the bed and sat on it, facing her.

"What's up?" He leaned closer to her, trying to catch her gaze, "Is this a medical thing I need to worry about? Should we be talking to a doctor?"

"Kind of. It's complicated."

"Okay, I'm listening,"

"First off, I want to apologize for never telling you this." Kim started, watching her husband's eyes, closely, as she spoke, "I thought I had dealt with it, but I guess I was wrong."

"Whatever it is, honey, it's…"

"No, no." She interrupted him, "Let me finish what I'm trying to say, please. I just want to get it out as simply and fast as I can. I bled because you hit a spot but it's not your fault, there is no way you would have known. The spot I'm talking about is an inflammation that has made my cervix tender. Sometimes, just using tampons can be hurtful talk less of sex."

"But it's not like this is our first time doing…"

"I know, I know. It doesn't happen like this usually. Most times, I bleed after we have sex. This time, it happened while we were going at it and it was even more painful than it usually is."

"How long have you known this?"

"Since I was a teenager."

"Honey, you're saying every time we have sex, you feel pain? You never said a word. We've been doing this for 3 years."

"I just got used to it." Kim said, "I got used to the pain. It's normal for me. I learnt how to manage the pain and the bleeding."

"This, this inflammation? What causes it? How can we get rid of it?"

"We can't."

He flung his hands in the air, "What do you mean we can't? Have you seen a doctor about this?'

"I've done more than just seeing a doctor. It's a condition and I know it. While I was completing my

Masters, I actually sought a doctor's help and after I had explained to the doctor about what I was feeling, he told me he had a hunch about why I was experiencing vaginal bleeding but I had to undergo laparoscopic surgery just so he could diagnose it and be sure that's really what it was. So, I had the surgery and he was right. I have endometriosis."

"What is that?" He pulled the sofa closer to her and grabbed her hands.

"You know how the tissue lining my uterus sheds when I'm on my period? With endometriosis, it's not just the uterus tissue lining that sheds; there's a tissue that awkwardly grows somewhere in my abdomen that sheds too but the blood and tissue can't leave my body, so it just causes more inflammation and pain. It keeps growing over time."

"Why didn't the doctor take care of it?"

"It's not that easy," Kim let out a heavy sigh, "You can't just get rid of it, the best you can do is stop it from triggering more pain. Plus, at the time, the spots of my endometriosis were too microscopic. So, I use… I use birth control pills to subdue the pain."

"You use birth control pills?" There was a look of shock on her husband's face, "Since when? How?"

"There are hormones in IUD birth control pills, the progestin-only ones, that help reduce the pain but the flip side of this is I don't have periods anymore and…"

"Honey, wait." He moved the sofa away and stood with arms akimbo, perplexed by the realization that his wife uses birth control pills, "Does this mean you've been delaying your own pregnancy? You never told me you were using pills. We've been trying to have a child for years, Kim. What are you really telling me here?"

She wanted to stand up, hold him and try to calm

him down but she couldn't muster the energy to do so. Instead, she sat still and stared at the floor.

"It's either that or endless pain." She said, "I had to do something to help myself live with the pain. It's not like I don't want a child, it's just I don't think my body can handle it.

"I can't believe you right now, Kim."

"I know, I know, I know." Kim didn't realize when she got teary and started sobbing, "I should have said something, but I was ashamed."

"I'm your husband for Christ's sake. What is there to be ashamed of?"

"There's more." Kim continued sobbing, "There's stuff I don't know how to say. I told you it's really complicated."

He dug his face in his palms and stayed far back away from her as he could. Kim looked up at him and in that instance, she knew the rest of the story would be too much for him to swallow. She decided she wasn't going to tell him the rest of it just yet.

"What else is there?" He finally asked.

"Nothing, it's just…I don't know if I can give birth to a child. I don't think I can. I mean I can, but it would be incredibly complicated to be pregnant with endometriosis. I don't think I can do it."

She broke into a series of blubbers. Deep down, she hoped he would come closer to hold and comfort her, but it didn't happen. Instead, the next thing he said broke her.

"I'm not sure I can do this." He said, "You hid this from me for three years, that's a long time to hide something this serious from someone you claim to love…I can't wrap my head around that. You haven't been fair to me/ You can see that, can't you?"

Kim didn't respond. She just continued sobbing.

"Can't you see you've been unfair to me, Kim?" He continued, "After three years of trying, you're telling me you've been taking birth control pills and we might not be able to have a child? That's just not fair. I… I need… to clear my head."

With that, he made his way to the exit.

"Where are you going?" She managed to ask, between sobs.

"I don't know." He grabbed his pajamas and opened the bedroom's door, "I just don't want to be anywhere close to you right now. You disgust me."

He slammed the door behind him.

FOUR

May 19, 2017

Speed breakers exist for two reasons: to enforce speed limits and to damage vehicles. That was Chris' opinion about them and no matter what anyone said, he was sticking with it. To him, speed breakers are the most pointless traffic calming measures to have ever been invented – right after speed tables.

Chris' disdain for speed breakers was at an all-time high, this morning, as he drove down St. Peter Street, driving over a speed breaker every ten seconds or at least, that's how long it seemed to him. The West End was developed partly due to the rapid growth the city experienced in the early 20th century. At the time, young people and newlyweds were flocking into the city like birds in the month of March.

The expansion was more than the city could handle so the city council decided to dedicate an insane amount of money into the development of a residential area, east of Route 62 and south of the Great River. It was a massive project that took two decades to complete. Due to its proximity to downtown, the area was very attractive to the newcomers and soon enough, it started getting overpopulated.

Years later, as the city developed, traffic calming measures had to be put in place to keep drivers in the popular and overpopulated West End in line – and Chris could swear that the speed breakers were the only traffic calming measure that was actually put in the place at the time. After all, there were way too many of them on a street like St. Peter. He once argued this theory with Beth.

"Why is it such a big deal to you?" Beth had been standing over the kitchen counter in her West End apartment, cooking mashed potatoes, "It's just speed bumps."

"They are everywhere for Christ's sake." Chris spoke loud enough for her to hear him, "You can't drive for ten seconds in the West End without bumping into one."

In his hand was the remote control for the television he was watching in her room. The kitchen was adjacent to the room but close enough for him to see her from the corner of her bed where he sat. Chris was about to lay insults on the city's mayor and his council when he shot a glance at her and got carried away by her free-flowing ebony-black hair as it cascaded down her back and rested on the slight curve in her behind. He shut his mouth, stood up, walked right into the kitchen and hugged her from behind.

"Oh, careful now." Beth hadn't seen him coming. "If you're going to talk trash about my neighborhood, you should know I have a knife in my hand."

"All I'm saying is," Chris continued, "One of you West End folks need to talk to your legislators about it – or maybe you guys are just blind to the fact."

"Again, I warn you I have a knife in my hand."

"Why do you think people who are well off are beginning to move away from these parts? They see what I see too."

Without turning around, Beth elbowed him and smiled as she heard him groan from behind.

"What does that mean?" She asked, "Are you saying I'm not well off?"

Chris pulled himself together, regained his stance, held her waist and slowly spun her around until her deep-set eyes were staring back at him.

"I mean, you have me." He spoke gently, "Of course, you're well off."

"You're so silly." She replied, with a sheepish grin and watched him come closer until they locked lips.

Just like that, Chris' thoughts had wandered from the speed breakers he was currently driving over to Beth's soft lips. Memories like that made his frequent trips to the West End worth it and this morning, he couldn't wait to start creating new memories with her. His days of contemplating if he was doing the right thing by being with her were gone and at the moment, he knew she was the one. She had to be.

Beth's apartment building was a four-storey structure that sat at the corner of St. Peter and Lethbridge. It was a sharp corner and a busy neighborhood, so Chris was sure to be extra careful as he parallel-parked his car across the street from the building. Less than a minute later, he was punching in Beth's buzzer code on an electronic panel that had been attached to the wall right beside the main entrance to the apartment building.

The panel let out a ringer and after waiting a few seconds, Chris could hear the building door unlock so he made his way in, rode an elevator to the fourth floor and as the elevator door opened up, he saw her – right there, already waiting.

"You're late." Beth's raised her eyebrows and shook her head. "We are going to be late."

Chris couldn't help but smile at her, then he reached out to grab the luggage in her right hand.

"It's not funny. You're always late." She said as she joined him in the elevator.

"You know what you remind me of?"

"I don't want to know." She looked away from him and directed the elevator to take them down to the apartment's lobby. "You said you would be here at…"

"When you said, 'You're late'," Chris interrupted her, "all I could think of was that scene from *License to Wed* where Robin William made the choir sing for what's his face, John Krasinski."

He ended his sentence with a loud, doltish laugh and it was contagious enough for Beth to break out of her mood to grin a little.

Chris began singing the song from the movie, and as he did, he edged closer to her and hugged her.

"I'm sorry." He said, "I would have gotten here much sooner if not for the stupid speed breakers you guys have lying around over here."

"Oh, come on." Beth slapped his chest, "Don't start."

"I've missed you, though." He tightened his hug, "I

really did."

"I missed you too."

"I've been looking forward to this trip all week, you know what I mean? Can you believe she was going to make me reschedule?"

"Come on, Chris, don't spoil the mood. Don't talk about her."

"Yeah, I won't. It's just... she pisses me off."

"Babe, you're not allowed to bring her up on this trip." Beth placed her palms on his cheeks and stared him in the eyes, "We have the weekend to ourselves and it should be all about us. We haven't had a trip like this in a while so let's enjoy it."

"Yeah, yeah, you're right. I promise not to mention her."

The elevator arrived at the lobby and they exited the building, crossed the street and started making their way to the airport. Chris drove as fast as the speed breakers would let him.

St. Peter street split into McDonald's avenue and Niakwa street – both routes lead to the airport but depending on the time of the day, one was usually faster than the other. Beth swore Niakwa street would take them less time, but Chris was certain that McDonald's was the thoroughfare of choice.

"You don't drive, how could you know which was faster?" Chris blurted out, as he turned the car into McDonald's avenue.

It only took about 30 seconds for him to start regretting those words. There was a slow-moving traffic on McDonald's avenue, and he had driven far enough that he could not turn around and head onto Niakwa street.

"Just say it," He said, without looking at Beth, "Just

say I told you so. I know you want to."

Beth shook her head, moved her hair to the side, revealing her sole birthmark – a bright spot that sat on her ebony face. She began tapping the spot, mildly and in a continuous, rhythmic, manner. It was her go-to move whenever she got frustrated.

"We are going to be late." She said, "You should have come earlier."

"We'll make it. We are just about ten minutes away; boarding doesn't start until half an hour."

"That's if we get through this traffic in ten minutes. I'm just glad I don't have to deal with you every day. I don't know how she does it."

Chris sank deeper into the car seat and let out a heavy sigh. This was supposed to be the beginning of a memorable weekend for both of them yet the morning – much like the traffic – wasn't looking too good at the moment. He had resolved that he was going to ignore what Beth had just said. She gets like this whenever she's anxious, he knew that and so, he wasn't going to let her drag him into an unnecessary row.

He was wrong about that.

"Why were you late, anyway?" Beth asked, visibly rattled, "You never said. Why were you late? I don't like being…"

"Beth," Chris was sure not to look in her direction, "We won't miss this flight, trust me and even if we do, we'll get on the next one. You don't need to get all panicky."

"Panicky?" Beth shifted slightly to get a proper look at him, "I'm not panicking. I'm just disappointed and really… Chris, to be honest, I'm just tired."

Now, she had his attention.

"What do you mean?" He turned his head towards her, "What does that even mean?"

"I can't keep doing this…" She started, "back and forth, juggling this and that, scheduling everything, hiding indoors… just being a goddamn afterthought, every time."

"Beth, you're not that. You're…"

"Then, why were you late?" Beth was beginning to raise her voice, "I can swear she had something to do with it."

"You said we shouldn't talk about her, yet you keep bringing her up."

"She's a freaking constant in everything. Whatever she does influences whatever we have. This - whatever you say we are – isn't going to move forward in any direction as long as she's right there."

"It's only a matter of time, Beth. I told you. We'll sort this. We just have to be really careful the way we go about it. I don't want people going about saying things about you – or me. You know what I mean? It's a small city, you know. Trust me, very soon, she'll be taken care of."

"You keep saying that, but I don't know." Beth was calmer now, "I don't know if this – us – means something, because I keep thinking that if it did, you would have done something about her. You're not even happy with her so what's the point?"

"For Christ's sake, Beth, she has no one. She's already a mess as it is. I have to be very careful the way I go about it. For now, she's my wife. Very soon, she won't be. Just trust me."

The car in front of them began moving so Chris regained control of the steering wheel and resumed driving. Using his left hand, he reached out towards

Beth and gently stroked her hair. She wasn't touching her birthmark anymore instead she wore a long face.

He understood how she felt. In the past year, they have had this conversation more times than he could count. It was the one uncolorful aspect of their relationship and this weekend, he was going to take care of it, once and for all.

PART TWO

The Burgess Theory

FIVE

May 20, 2017

Of course, I miss them.

They've been gone for a while now, but you know, there are all these memories that never go away. Everyone deals with some kind of loss at some point in their lifetime but to lose your parents at a very young age – especially when you don't fully understand what death is – it's extra sensitive.

I'm not sure how I dealt with mine, but I know my sister played a big role in helping me get through that season of my life. She was the one true family I had left; I mean I had my aunt for a while, but she also passed away like two years after my parents.

To be honest, I thought I was going to go too. I really did. I was 15 years old when my aunt died – we called her aunt Tolani –and at that age, having lost three adults in my life, I didn't think I was going to be an exception. Somewhere at the back of my mind, I believed that adults in my family were bound to die. I was expecting some of my uncles and aunts back home to die as well. I even thought that once I became a grown-up, I would die.

Yes, it was a stupid phase of my life, but it wasn't unfounded. Death had taken those closest to me in a quick and very unexpected manner, so I began to expect it to show up at my doorsteps any time. My mind was just programmed to think that way. It took me a while – even as an adult – to dissociate myself from that way of thinking, you know what I mean?

How did my parents die?

Oh, it was a plane crash. I remember it like it was yesterday. We were visiting a city in my home country called Port Harcourt for Christmas, but my parents sent my sister and me to go ahead of them. Aunt Tolani was with us anyway so we were good. My parents were supposed to join us the next day – oh god, it's crazy how I remember this so vividly.

On the day of the crash, my sister and I were watching the television in the hotel room we had lodged into. Aunt Tolani had stepped out to get something – I can't remember what it was, but it took her a while before she got back. Anyway, one of us decided to switch up the channels and on the next station, the broadcaster was talking about a plane crash that had just happened at the Port Harcourt International Airport.

Ade – that's my sister's name, by the way – was nagging me about changing the station, you know, but for some reason, I was intrigued by the details of the crash. I wanted to know how and why it happened, so I stayed glued to the screen. It was all very fascinating until I heard the broadcaster say their names.

Just imagine what that looks like; a 13-year-old finding out about his parents' death through a news broadcast. It was crazy. We both heard it – my sister and I – we both heard it and we immediately knew what it meant. We knew they were gone. Ade started crying right there and then. I didn't cry immediately so I tried to console her. Not too long after that, aunt Tolani returned from wherever she was, and I had to deliver the news to her myself. She didn't believe until she checked out the broadcast herself. It was…

Who is older? We're twins – ha-ha, sure, sure, sure. She came out first so yeah, she is.

Anyway, that day was the beginning of the topsy-turvy ride that has been my life. Somethings happened back home with our extended family and Ade and I were going to be displaced so Aunt Tolani decided to take us in and that's how we got the chance to move to Canada with her, you know what I mean? She lived there but would come back to visit so after that Christmas, she just took us in.

Who? Aunt Tolani?

Damn, she is a long story.

Ha-ha, I mean it. She is.

Our relationship – aunt Tolani and I – our relationship was quite, I don't know, interesting. I don't want to go into details, you might get grossed out and understandably so.

Yeah, yeah, I know you will. You definitely would. It's one of those things people frown on but I didn't, and I still don't.

No, no, no, I'm not sharing that. I want to honor the dead. She was a sweet lady and she died way too young. She was only 30 years old when she died.

Can you imagine that? She was so…

Why do you keep asking that?

Alright sure, I will say this much. My aunt and I, we had some sort of – I don't know – an intimate relationship. Something like that.

What do I mean by that?

Well, we were pretty close. I feel like she was one person who really understood and saw me, you know what I mean? My parents were socialites back home, so they had all these expectations and responsibilities that just kind of followed them wherever they went. Somehow, that also meant that my sister and I had to behave in a certain way to keep our parents' reputation intact. They didn't let us express ourselves but with Aunt Tolani, I could be myself.

Back then, every time aunt Tolani visited home from Canada, my mum would prepare our guest room for her. The room was right beside mine. Sometimes, I would have nightmares – and usually, when that happens, I would run to my mom's room – but whenever aunt Tolani was around, I would go to the guest room instead. She would let me sleep with her and make sure that I felt very comfortable. That's how we got pretty close.

I know what you're thinking and the answer is yes. We got that close. I didn't mind it at the time and even now, as I'm saying this to you – I don't see anything wrong with it, but I know many people would be, you know, irked by it. I wasn't forced to do anything I didn't want to. It just happened. I felt safe and at peace with her as a kid.

The simple truth is Aunt Tolani was my first, you know what I mean? Yes, she was. I lost my virginity to her.

No, she didn't use me. I wouldn't say she did. She really didn't. I knew what was going on and I let it happen. It's crazy that I'm telling you this. I've never shared this with anyone. This is nuts. You're going to have to tell me something crazy about you too. This has to go both ways. You can't just sit there listening to me tell you crazy stories.

Okay, this is done. I'm going to roll a new blunt. You want one?

Do I miss her? Of course, I do.

I honestly felt like she was my first love, you know. She was pure and just very – what's the word for it? – homely in a good way, you know what I mean? I like to think I made her feel that way too. Yeah, I was young and, you know, naïve to an extent but I like to think I was there for her. I feel like she felt safe with me – like, emotionally, you know what I mean?

It started with bedtime stories. I was the type of kid who couldn't go to bed without listening to some sort of lullaby or reading a bedtime story, you know what I mean? Ade wasn't like that. She could go to bed by just thinking about it.

Usually, my mum would stay up with me, in my bedroom, reading bedtime stories to me so I could fall asleep but whenever aunt Tolani came to visit on one of those long holidays, my mum would ask her to read me those stories instead. That was how we formed a unique connection. We would go from just reading the stories to having conversations about things going on with me at school and how she was navigating work and relationships. She always said I was the wisest teenager she ever met but technically, I wasn't a teenager when we started hanging out or whatever.

Our conversations would go on late into the night and eventually I would fall asleep on her lap. It kind of started like that, you know. One night, she asked me... and by the way, she always asked me before we did anything, you know? That's why I'm sure everything we did was cordial or consensual – whatever the hell the word is. Anyway, one night after we were done with the bedtime story, she asked me if I wanted her to stay there with me and I said yes. So, she grabbed a duvet and we got underneath it. We laid side to side staring at each other under the very, you know, dimly lit duvet. I remember she wore this smile on her face that made me feel a sense of warmth.

Ha-ha, no, no, it wasn't the duvet.

Listen, this is a feeling I can't even explain – that's how you know it was quite deep. Anyway, she moved my left hand and placed it on her warm cheek. Then, slowly she moved it down until we got to one of her breasts – I played with it a bit – but we didn't stop there. At that point, we had moved just inches away from each other, I could feel her skin on mine, but the very best feeling came when she made me finger her. Her face lit up with euphoria as I felt the warmth of her vagina. That's how I knew she liked it and as a kid, who was in love with this woman, I wanted her to always feel that way.

After that night, every time we got together, we would do it all over again. It went from fingering her to her making me come and then eventually, we actually started having sex. We did for years – till she died.

No, I don't think anyone else knew. Not even my sister.

Although, there was a night we were underneath the duvet, and someone walked into my room. It might have been my mum. I don't know but I know I heard someone walk in and then walk out. If it was my mum, then she never said a word about it to me. I don't know – maybe I'm just remembering things wrong.

Molested? Ha-ha, that isn't molestation. I know what molestation is. What I had with aunt Tolani isn't molestation.

No, you're wrong. She didn't use me. She loved me. I loved her. That's it.

I don't know why I'm telling you any of this. I'm just going to shut the hell up.

SIX

February 16, 2017

"I don't know where he is." Kim paced the room as she spoke into her phone, "He didn't come back home last night. He's not picking my calls. I'm getting worried."

She put the phone on speaker mode and set it down on her kitchen counter, then proceeded to tap the screen, making selections until she found her husband's office number. It's been almost 12 hours since he walked out on her, leaving her with the echoes of those three words that you never want to hear from someone you love – "You disgust me."

He wasn't the kind of man who made those remarks without giving it some amount of thoughts. The weight of those words wasn't lost on him and he knew better than to act with insolence towards her or hurl hurtful words at her. If anything, she needed him to be there to tell her that everything would be alright. She had torn down her walls and tried to be vulnerable with him by telling him about her endometriosis. The least he could do is acknowledge that.

After he left last night, she rang his cell a few times but when she realized that he wasn't going to pick up her calls, she curled herself into a ball and cried until she fell asleep. The sharp rays of sunlight, that ripped through her curtains and landed on her forehead, woke her up early this morning. She turned around to his side of the bed and he wasn't there. That's when she got panicky.

Kim jumped off the bed and ran into the bathroom to check if he was in there. He wasn't. She raced downstairs and combed the square feet of her house – including the garage and backyards. He wasn't there. His car wasn't, either. She resorted to using her phone to keep dialing and redialing him.

In the middle of her frantic and chaotic morning, she got a call from her friend, Amina. There was no better person to give her a call at that moment. Amina was the one person Kim could be completely open with. She knew just about everything that there was to know about Kim. They've been as stick as thieves since they were little girls and regardless of how far – and completely different – life's path had taken them, their bond never grew weak instead their friendship has blossomed and weathered the toughest times. They were more than your regular old skin and blister – they were family. The only family Kim could trust with everything, even her husband didn't know her as much as Amina did.

"Why do you sound like you've been crying?" Amina immediately asked after Kim picked up her call. "Are you okay?"

On hearing Amina's voice, Kim couldn't resist the urge to blub her eyes out. She started crying again and spoke in an incoherent manner as if she was picking at the words.

"Kim, you're crying. What's wrong?"

"He isn't back home," Kim started, "He isn't picking my calls either."

"Alright, I'm going to need you to calm down and speak slowly." Amina's voice grew stern as she spoke, "When did he leave? Do you any idea where he could be? Maybe a friend's place?"

"I don't know where he is. He didn't come back home last night. He's not picking my calls. I'm getting worried."

"Okay Kim, listen to me." Amina began scolding her, "What the hell are you doing crying? When did you become this person? Play smart and think logically. Have you called his friends? Or his office? Better yet, if he isn't picking, maybe he wants his space and you should probably just give him space and time. I'm talking to you, what are you doing?"

"I'm searching for his office's number." Kim tried to speak clearly so her voice could be audible over the speakerphone. "You said I should check his office or friends."

"Forget that," Amina shut back, "Go sit your ass down somewhere and tell me what happened. We both know he's not the type to just ghost you. He probably just needs some time to think. So, tell me what's going on."

Kim followed suit. She picked up her phone from

the countertop, found her way to the living room and planted herself on the couch.

"Tell me what happened?" Amina continued, "He didn't hit you right? I know he wouldn't do that to you."

"No, he didn't." Kim replied, "I think it was my fault."

"What did you do?"

"I told him. I shouldn't have told him."

"What did you tell him?" Amina asked, obviously frustrated by Kim's half-empty replies, "Just tell me what happened from the top."

"We were having sex, right…"

"Okay, go on."

"Then, I started bleeding." Kim continued, "The bleeding usually happens after the fact but this time, it happened before we were done. It really hurts this time and I started crying. I wish I didn't. I shouldn't have cried… I shouldn't…."

"It happens, Kim." Amina cut in, "You can't control that. You can't control your endometriosis. I'm just going to go on a limb and guess that you guys finally had the conversation? Right?"

"Yeah, we did. Just half of it."

"What part did you leave out?"

"I didn't leave it out. I was going to tell him, but he walked out. He got mad about the birth control pills."

"Shit!" Amina blurted out, "I forgot about those. Oh crap, of course, he's mad. Shit, shit."

"I don't know what to do."

Kim went back into sobbing mode much to Amina's disdain.

"Kim, crying isn't going to do anything for you." Amina said, "Stay calm, I'm sure he'll be back. Does he know about the guy?"

"No, I didn't get to that part."

"Okay, Kim. You know what you need to do when he gets back?"

"If he gets back…" Kim interrupted Amina's suggestion, "We don't know if he's…"

Amina returned the favour, "Woman, would you just relax for a second. It's not even up to a day. Relax, he'll be back and when he's back, you need to tell him everything – all of it. Don't leave any details out."

"I don't think he can handle it, Amina."

"He can – and even if he doesn't, at least you would have done your part. Listen to me, girl. I have told you for years. None of this – endometriosis or the other shit – none of it is your fault. You don't deserve it, but it happened to you, now you have to deal with it like a queen. Hold your head up high and keep carrying on. I need you to do that."

"Amina, it's easy for you to say." As Kim spoke these words, she heard the sound of car drive into her driveway, "Wait, I think he's here."

With that, Kim stood up and peered through the curtains. A taxi was parked in her driveway and out of it, came her husband. He still had his pajamas on as he staggered towards their front door.

"He's here, Amina. I'm going to have to call you back."

"Alright. Remember, you're a queen so…"

Kim cancelled the call before Amina could complete her sentence. She unlocked the door and opened it to meet him dangling his keys – he'd been obviously trying to find the right key to open the door before she got to it.

The first thing she noticed was that he reeked of

alcohol. He'd been drinking and the stench lingered with him. She reached out to hugged him. To her surprise, he met her halfway. This brought tears to her eyes.

"I'm so sorry, honey," She repeated, "I'm sorry. I should have told you."

Together, they walked to the couch and sat on it. He had one hand wrapped around her shoulder and the other held her head close to his chest. They shared a moment together and at some point, Kim muttered, "I love you and I'm sorry."

"I love you too," He replied.

"I'm so sorry," Kim repeated.

"Kim," He caressed her head as he spoke, "You said there's more you have to say."

She nodded slowly to reply.

"Okay," He continued, "do you want to tell me what else I need to know?"

"Sure, I will."

She raised her head from his chest, and he helped her straighten herself up and wipe the tears off her face.

When she was good to go, she continued, "My bleeding didn't start until I go to college. I was a freshman when it started – it was my very first semester. At that point, I was just happy to be away from my parents' home – I finally had some sense of freedom. So, I was really just a happy-go-lucky champ. I would party every weekend. Amina and I, we would always keep our eyes peeled for any opportunities for us to have a good time.

"This one time, we heard about a Halloween party. Of course, being that it was a Halloween party, we had to wear costumes or, at least, masks. I wore a mask and a dress. People at this party couldn't really see each other. I was having a good time until this guy asked me to dance with him. At first, I wasn't interested. I was with Amina and we were doing our thing, but he kept coming around and eventually, Amina said I could just go on with him. Some other guy was asking her to dance with him anyway, so we went our separate ways. I was dancing with this guy and we started getting pretty intimate with it. At some point, we were kissing on the dance floor. I was into it – we were both just having fun. I mean it was a Halloween party so you know how those can be – just crazy.

"It really, really, got crazy when he whispered in my ears and asked me if I was down for some weed. I might have said, yes. I don't know. All I remember after that is, we were at the back of the building – in an alley – and he was rolling a blunt. We smoked together and started making out. We kept going at it and I knew, at a point, that we were going to have sex – and to be honest, I was fine with that, but I didn't expect what this guy did next.

"With his right hand, while we were still making out, he reached into my pants and dipped his fingers – it really felt like it was all five of them – into my vagina. He just kept ramming into it with his fingers. It felt like someone was unscrewing something inside of me. It hurt badly. I told him he was hurting me and asked him to stop but he didn't. Instead, he went at it with even more force. I tried to scream but before I knew it, his other palm was right there, covering my mouth. I was just there with my back against this brick wall in this dimly lit alley. I was making muffled sounds and crying but with the loud music blaring from the party that was going on inside, no one could hear me.

"After a while, I just let him do what he wanted to

do. It was the weirdest thing…"

"Oh my god, Kim." He held her close and said, "I'm so sorry. This is nuts. That must have been devastating for you. Listen, if you don't want to talk about it, we can do this later…"

"No," Kim shrugged, "I want to do this now. It's long overdue. Just let me get through what I'm saying then we can talk. Okay?"

He nodded.

"By the time he was done fingering me, I was jso weak and in pain. I stumbled over and laid on the ground, then he got on top of me and finished me off. That part took a few seconds and when he was done, he zipped himself up, went right back into the party and left me lying there. As I laid there, I thought that was it for me. I thought I was going to die. I couldn't move and frankly, I didn't want to. A part of me was wishing that whatever he was did to me would somehow kill me. I laid there for maybe half an hour before Amina found me. By the time she got there, I was seriously bleeding. She called an ambulance and when the paramedics came by, the entire party had to be shut down. I was rushed to the hospital and administered all sorts of blood treatments just to help me regain my energy and consciousness.

"The doctor and nurses kept asking me what happened, but I couldn't bring myself to even acknowledge, let alone talk about it. Amina had a clue, but I shut her down whenever she tried to speak of it. It wasn't until a month after I was out of that hospital that I confided in her and told her what had happened. She was furious – very much so because she had a hunch, but I had been denying it."

"Who else knows about this?" He asked,

"No one, just Amina. I can't bring myself to say a word of this to anyone. I just had to muster the courage to say it to you. I don't want you to look at me in any…"

"Honey, how can you say that?" He leaned in, kissed her, then he hugged her. With his mouth directly beside her right ear, he said, "What's the point of what we have if we can't share this? There is no such thing as shame between us. Whatever affects you, affects me. You should know that by now."

"I know but it's not easy to actually think that way when it comes to something like this." She said, "This was something I tried to hide from everyone. For a long time, I didn't want to believe that it actually happened, so I never spoke about it."

"I understand," He removed himself from the hug, "So, I'm guessing this had something to do with the other thing?"

Kim nodded, "I think so. I don't know for a fact but after the incidence, I noticed that I would feel so much pain when I menstruate. The pain got worse whenever I would have sex and eventually, when I had it checked out, I was told that it's endometriosis. I'm going to need you to actually say that word next time, honey. Don't just say the 'thing'."

"Sure, sure, endometriosis. I'm sorry, it's just a lot to take in."

"I know but now you know."

"So, what can we do?" He asked, "How can we figure out a way to help you feel better? Are we ever going to be able to have a child?"

"I don't know, honey." Kim sighed, "Since we are both aware of this now, maybe together we could seek help from a doctor or something?"

"Yeah, we could talk to the family doctor. He might be able to refer us to a specialist."

"Yeah, he might. Before we do that though, there's something I have to do."

"What's that?"

"There's someone I have to talk to."

SEVEN

May 19, 2017

The plane landed shortly after noon. Just in time for them to pick up the rental car they had booked and be on their way to Harmony Park Music Garden. The garden sat at the shore of Geneva Lake and was about an hour away from Rochester International Airport.

Somewhere in Mapleview and halfway from the garden, Chris strapped himself back into the driver seat and waited for Beth to appear from the roadside gas bar and convenience store they had stopped by to fill up. He glanced at his phone. It had the Google Maps app open so he tried to memorize the next few turns he would have to make before they arrived at their destination.

Barring a few sharp curves here and there, Route 90

was a pretty straightforward highway and if you were heading to Geneva, it was even easier. All you really had to do was take the exit 159B to merge onto Route 35 as if you're heading out to Minneapolis/St. Paul. A quick bend onto Route 25 will take you towards Clark Groove and soon you would be at the Geneva Township. It shouldn't take you too long to find the lake and of course, the garden.

As usual, the garden was the venue for the annual Noble Music Festival and this three day-festival was Chris' and Beth's rendezvous for the weekend. They had met there a year ago so they figured it would be the best meeting place to celebrate the one-year anniversary of their somewhat classified relationship.

Before agreeing to come on the trip, Beth had laughed at Chris' suggestion of some sort of anniversary celebration.

"We are not even dating." Beth had said to Chris, "What would we be celebrating?"

"A year together." The words fell right off Chris' lips, "We have something special and I want us to make it a habit to be grateful for it."

"Babe, I agree that we have something special, but we aren't really tapping into it and we can barely quantify what we have as a relationship. Whenever you go back home, you go back into the arms of another woman. I'm a mistress – and I know that."

"You're not." Chris quickly rebutted, "You're not a mistress. You're the love of my life and I want to celebrate you, celebrate us, celebrate this."

"You like to act like you live in denial or like you don't understand the basics of how things work. You can't celebrate something that doesn't exist. You never asked me out. You never made me your girlfriend. We met each other at the festival last year, started hanging out when we got back to the city and ending up boning each other on the regular."

"Don't do that, Beth." Chris said, "Don't act like there are no strings attached here. Don't belittle what we here."

"I'm not belittling anything, babe," Realizing that the conversation was getting a bit more serious, she shot a glance at him, "All I'm saying is we are not official so we can't officially celebrate."

"Whatever you say. That shouldn't stop us from planning a weekend away."

"Minnesota is barely away, babe."

Beth was right. Minnesota was barely away but it was far enough for Chris to get away from his wife and the suspicion and gazes that could result from hanging out in public with Beth back in the city. After this weekend, none of that would matter. He would make what he has with Beth official – so official that it would be worthy of a ceremony.

Shortly after, Beth emerged out of the convenience store and got back into the car. They continued their trip to the garden. About 30 minutes later, Chris parked the rental car in a parking lot, a very short distance away from the garden and Geneva Lake. The lot was packed and from where they stood, they could see people setting up tents and laying down picnic blankets. It was just day one of the festival, yet the garden was chock-full with music lovers.

"When does Kaiser go on stage?" Beth asked, as she grabbed their picnic blanket and basket from the trunk,

"I think they are on at nine pm. I may be wrong."

"That's the session I'm really waiting for."

"You listened to their new album?" Chris joined her

to grab their stuff from the trunk.

"Of course, I have. It's so amazing, Chris. I love it so much. They just keep getting better."

"I think so too. I think this is their best project yet."

"I heard Williams is leaving the band though." Beth closed the trunk, set the items down and straightened the headscarf she had on.

"Who's Williams? The drummer?"

"No, he's the bass guitarist."

"Really? That unfortunate. He's really good. Why is he leaving?"

"No idea, it might just be a rumor though."

"I guess we will find out today." Chris concluded.

Waves of folk music filled the open space where campers and music lovers had gathered at the garden. Chris found a spot up the hill and close to the lake. Together, they set down their picnic basket and blanket and made the space theirs. From their vantage point, they could see the stage and recognize the faces of those who performed on it.

The music continued into the evening as band after band took turns to perform and serenade the crowd. The arrival of sunset was met with an increase in headcounts at the garden and a corresponding increase in noise or music levels – depending on which sound you made more attention to. Chris and Beth did their best to play their part by raising their voices every now and then to cheer the stage performers or just sing along with them.

As the evening wore on, Chris prepped himself. He had it all planned out in his head. He was already at the perfect spot, he just had to do it at the perfect time. Many at times, people would visit the garden to take pictures of the scenic setting and views but on a day like this, with people covering almost every inch of the garden, it was quite difficult to capture those kinds of pictures. Chris didn't mind – the photographer he had recruited wasn't hired for landscape pictures. From the corner of his eyes, he could see the photographer lingering by the lake waiting for the signal to move.

Chris panned around to take in the sights and one by one, he could see the members of the flash mob he had hired all in their positions – acting like regular festival attendees but really – waiting to make their moves. He glanced at his watch. Five minutes to go.

A couple minutes later, the band on stage ended their set and an announcer walked up to the mic to declare the next hour as a break in transmission. Just as Chris had predicted, the festivities would resume by nine pm and at eight pm, the charades he had planned could begin. And it did.

It began with a loud female voice singing the lyrics of *One Republic*'s "All this Time". As she wrapped up the first verse, a guitarist joined her to usher in the chorus and before they were done with the chorus, drums could be heard guiding them along as they moved along the beat. More people joined the female singer for the second verse and with each new line, more voices could be heard and then, the choreography began.

At this point, a visibly elated Beth had figured out that it was a flash mob, but she didn't know what they were there for or what they were calling attention to. Her smile widened as she bopped her head from side to side watching more people join the mob. It wasn't until she shot a glance at Chris that she realized what was going on. He was on one knee and had a small box stretched out towards her.

"Oh my God! "She caught herself mid-gasp and covered her mouth with both palms.

It all made sense to her now. Chris had chosen the festival and that particular space, up the hill, all because of this moment. As she put the pieces together in her head, the singing-voices began to subside and what followed were loud cheers from the regular festival goers who were watching eagerly to see how this moment would unfold.

She could see Chris' lips moving. He was saying something, but she could barely hear him. The more he spoke, the louder the cheers got and in the middle of all that, she could feel rapid flashes from a camera's flashlight somewhere around her. She knew that a proposal was supposed to be a memorable and beautiful moment but right now, all she could feel was chaos. It was loud, bright and intense. Something about this didn't seem right – and the chaos around her was just an offshoot of an anomaly deeply rooted in the nature of their relationship.

Chris.

Beth stared at him as he spoke. Tears began to roll down her cheeks as she realized he was about to wrap up whatever he was saying. She wanted to scream and tell him to stop and take it all back. The scream didn't come instead it was whispers and rapid left-to-right-and-back movements of her head that sufficed.

Chris' face went from glee to confusion when he noticed her head movements. She was saying no. He couldn't believe it – how could she? She had always hinted at this. She always nagged about not being number one in his life. She always questioned his motives with her and here he was, making a grand gesture of commitment, on a hill, in the presence of thousands of people. How could she say no?

"Beth?" Chris' eyebrows furrowed slight, "What are you doing? Just say yes."

"I can't." She continued whispering, "I just can't. This isn't right. I'm so sorry. I'm so sorry. I just…"

With that, she grabbed the car key that laid on the picnic blanket and darted off the hill towards the parking lot. She could hear the groans and sighs around her as she raced away. It was such a surreal moment, she wished all of this was a nightmare but the further she ran against the force of the evening's breeze, the more she knew it was real. She had just made a choice that would have a massive impact on her relationship and life. This was something that she would never be able to forget. It all happened so fast – and yet, it wasn't over.

As Beth got closer to where the car was parked, she could hear footsteps behind her. They were loud and on par with hers. She was being chased but was too scared to look back, so she didn't. She just kept running. Barring the lines of parked cars, the parking lot was dark and empty. It made it a lot difficult for Beth to navigate her way through it. She pressed the unlock button on the car's remote key and that caused the car's headlight to flash on. Now she knew where she was going. She took a shortcut and walked through the space between two cars.

As soon as she walked out of the space, she heard Chris' voice from behind her.

"Where are you going? I thought this was what you wanted?"

"I'm sorry." She halted and turned around, "I can't do this. I just can't."

"Really, Beth?" Chris had been running behind her,

so he tried to catch his breath before he continued speaking, "This is what you wanted. I'm giving you what you want."

"No," Her voice was hoarse from crying, "I thought I wanted this, but I don't. I really don't. I don't want to be with you."

"You don't want to be with me?" Chris was beginning to raise his voice, "What are you saying right now? What are you actually saying? You don't want to be with me? How did we go from one thing to this?"

"Chris, I know you. I've tried to act like I don't know that part of you doesn't exist, but it does."

"What are you talking about, Beth. This doesn't have to be this difficult. We can talk about this. Surely, we can."

Beth began walking backwards towards the next line of cars, he followed her and kept a short distance between them.

"Chris, you can't be a good husband." Still walking away and backwards, she said, "Once I say yes, you would start taking me for granted just like you take her for granted."

"Why in the world do you keep bringing her into everything?" He yelled, "What we have has nothing to do with her."

"No, Chris. It does. Everything about this has to do with her. You're not good to her and you can't be good to me. You will hurt me just like you hurt her. I can't let you do that to me."

The more she spoke, the more visibly furious he got. She could tell that that he was trying to keep himself together.

"You are nothing like her, Beth. You don't have to compare yourself with her in any way."

"Chris," She arrived at the bonnet of a silver Honda, two cars away from Chris' "Don't make me say it."

"Say what?"

"You rape her. We both know this. You're a rapist. I can't be with you. I shouldn't."

"No, no, no, no, you don't mean that." Chris clenched his fist and marched faster towards her, "You don't mean that, Beth. Don't say that."

"You're a rapist!" She repeated and hastened her steps backwards, "You're a rapist!"

She slipped and fell over, landing backwards beside the rear tires of the silver Honda. Chris used that opportunity to get a hold of her. He grabbed her by the arm, pulled her back up, pinned her against the silver Honda, and covered her mouth with his left palm.

"Don't say that." Chris' eyes dilated

"You're a rapist! You're a rapist!" Beth didn't relent, she kept screaming and kicking with all the energy she could muster.

"Beth, stop it!"

Realizing that he couldn't keep her down for long, Chris went for her neck and held it tightly, causing her muffled voice to change to wheezing sounds. Yet, she didn't stop kicking at him – eventually, the heel of her feet struck his genitals. He jerked backwards and released her from his grip. She took advantage of his imbalance and tried to strike him one more time, but his reflexes were too quick for her. He caught her leg mid-air, pushed her back towards the car, grabbed her long hair, pulled it towards him then gripped the back of head and pushed it back towards the car. Her head landed heavily on the trunk and she fell backwards hitting her head on the ground, this time.

Chris, still breathing heavily, stared at Beth's body on the ground. He quickly looked around – the parking lot was still empty, no one but cars in sight – and then, he bent down beside her, grabbed her arm and checked her pulse but he couldn't feel anything. Without thinking twice, he took the car key out of her hand, lifted her weight off the ground, and with Beth's body over his right shoulder, he ran towards his car and unlocked the trunk.

There was little to nothing he could do, at this point. He didn't have many options. She had been seen with him at the garden so if anyone found her body lying around anywhere close to the garden, they would trail it back to him. He had to find a way to take care of her body. He lifted her off his shoulder and laid her in the trunk then he got into the driver seat and darted off.

As Chris' car turned out of the lot and onto the highway, the engine of one of the cars in the parking lot revved on. The car reversed out of its parked position and its driver bolted out of the lot – keeping a safe distance between it and Chris' car.

EIGHT

May 20, 2017

Now that I think of it, I think my mum knew.

I think she did. I remember every now and then, my mum would have an argument with aunt Tolani about me. Aunt Tolani always felt like my mum was really hard on me – and to be honest, that might have been true – but, you know, they would go back and forth about it. My guess is my mum had a hunch about it and if she did, she never said a word to me about it but she might have given her a lot of stick.

My mum was always busy, you know. She always had something going on. She didn't have much time for us. I understood it – she was a socialite and there was always a maid around to help us. So, I didn't mind, you know? I wish I spent more time with her but it's whatever, you know? She's gone now and wishes aren't pennies.

Losing family at a young age helped me to learn how to navigate life on my own – well, with my sister. I had to learn to do what it takes to protect myself. I mean it, I had to. After my aunt died, we were stranded. Two kids without a guardian, that's just nuts, you know what I mean?

So, of course, social workers picked us up and dropped us with the first foster family who didn't mind having two black immigrants kids to boss around while pocketing a monthly paycheck.

Our first foster parents were these two old folks who lived about 2 hours away from the city. Well, I shouldn't say old – the man was in his fifties, but the wife was in late thirties at the time, but they had been married for, I think, maybe two decades. They couldn't have kids for some reason, I don't remember why. Some medical reason, you know what I mean?

Being in a foster home is really like being in a makeshift family, you know what I mean? We knew it wasn't real. We knew they couldn't really love us as their own. It was just an arrangement. They got paid to provide a bed for us to sleep on each night and frankly, we were fine with that. All they had to do was make sure we had a place to sleep but it got really tricky when they tried to get more involved with us. I'll tell you why.

As a kid, who had just lost three instrumental and close family members, I have an image of what a parent or loved one should look like. You know what I mean? The image is just there – ingrained in my head – and I know it, but these people were strangers. They didn't look, speak or act like me. They were Caucasians, I'm black. You know what I mean? Even at age 15, the difference was clear. Subtle but clear.

Bottom line is they had expectations about certain things that I couldn't meet. They wanted me to act in a certain way, but I wasn't sure about living my life that way.

What's that? I should give you an example. Sure, I'll give you one.

These guys were staunch Christians. I mean the type who serve on a Sunday morning, dress to their toes and go on hilltops to pray. They held a position in the church – deacons – or something like that. As far as they were concerned, their way of life guaranteed them a straight pass into heaven or what not.

No, I'm not talking about the Joseph Smith believers. These were your everyday Christian folks – but quite extreme with the way they went about it.

They tried to impose their way of life on my sister and me. We didn't grow up in the church, so we weren't familiar with these things. They would try to get us to wake up early on a Sunday morning to head out to church, and at the dinner table, if you didn't say the grace before you started eating, you could get spanked. Literally. In fact, they believed that if you didn't pour some kind of ointment on your head before stepping out of the house in the morning, then you would be to blame if anything bad happened to you that day.

Yes, that extreme.

The man would spank me every now and then, whenever he caught me watching a television station with contents that they, as a couple, have decided was sinful. I got used to the spanking because there was always something, quote on quote, "sinful" that I got myself into without even know that it was sinful. I was just a kid, what the hell did I know?

At first, I thought I wouldn't survive my time at the house because I couldn't handle the rules and general culture of the household. I was kind of wrong because I ended up finding solace in the arms of the wife instead. The man would spank me and get mad at me but then I would run to the wife, who would speak softly to me, correct me by telling me what I did wrong and advise me on the right thing to do.

She was good to me that way, you know what I mean?

No, no, no, not in that way. Not like aunt Tolani. More like a compassionate teacher. Someone you could talk to and they could help you navigate through life. She was still a stranger to me – not family – but I found some comfort in the warmth of this particular stranger. She was the Ying to her husband's Yang. He could get abusive but she, she was pure and amiable. They complemented each other.

Sometimes he would spank me for things he deemed sinful, so I would run away from the house for a couple of days. I'd just go someplace and sleep – sometimes at my friend's place. It was a small town so eventually, they would fish me out, take me back home and he would give me another round of spanking. After getting spanked, his wife would take me aside and try to cheer me up. Sometimes, I wonder if they were both in on it – you know, like good cop, bad cop. Who knows?

One morning, I got into a heated argument with him. He had declared that day as a day of fasting in the house. You know what I mean?

Not really?

Well, it means you can't have a meal or eat anything

at all throughout that day until about six pm in the evening. I thought it was a crazy thing to ask me to do that – especially as someone who didn't understand the reason for doing it. He wanted us to fast till six pm and I tried to tell that I couldn't do it. He insisted that everyone living under his roof had to do it.

"There are some prayers that can only be answered by collective prayers and fasting." He kept repeating that to me.

I didn't understand it. Anyway, on the day we were supposed to fast, I woke up early for school and made myself a sandwich. I knew I wasn't supposed to do that, given his instructions, but I didn't care. None of it made sense to me. I sat on the dining table and munched my breakfast sandwich, without a care in the world. I knew I would get into trouble for doing so but I didn't care about getting spanked. I was kind of used to it, you know what I mean?

Well, of course, he caught me having that breakfast and he got mad about it. He kept yelling that I had sinned, and that God wouldn't listen to my prayers because I hadn't kept my end of the bargain by fasting.

"I'm not interested in any sort of bargain with God," I said to him,

"As long as you're in this house, you have to live under God's covenant and do as He says. If He says you should fast, then you must fast." He yelled at me and then went on a tirade about disobedience being a sin – citing King Saul as an example. As he spoke, he got really steamed up and before I knew it, he pulled out his belt and started flinging it at me. He struck me numerous times with that belt. His wife and my sister came and tried to stop him, but he was quick to shove them to the side.

As if the belt wasn't enough, he started throwing punches at me. I tried to keep my cool and just take it in. I wasn't raised to hit adults or talk back to them, so I was doing my best to keep my mouth and hands to myself. He gave me a red eye that morning and grounded me for the rest of the day. So, I spent that day at home – locked in my room.

Later that afternoon, his wife walked into the room with a wet towel, bowl of water and an ice pack to help reduce the redness and swelling around my eye. Then, we got talking. It was one of the most eye-opening conversations I have ever had.

"I'm sorry you had to go through that," She said as she handed me the ice pack, "He gets furious when he feels like he isn't being heard or understood."

"I don't feel like I'm being understood too." I shot back at her, "Listen, I appreciate all that the both of you do for my sister and me but I'm not sure we signed up for this part. I could easily report these things to the social worker assigned to our case, but I think about…"

She looked at me, agog to hear the end of my statement but I didn't complete it so she asked, "Why haven't you?"

You see, I had never admitted the answer to that question to myself until I said it out loud that day. When I said it, I realized how much it meant to me to have this woman in my life.

"You." I answered her, "You're the reason I haven't reported this. I know you guys could use the check you get for this. I know you guys struggle to keep a roof over our heads and I know you, particularly, wish you could have children of your own. I know that with Ade and me being here, it gives you that opportunity to live like you have kids. So, yeah, it's you. I feel for you and you've been good to me. I don't think you deserve to have us taken away from you."

She already began crying before I was done speaking. I tried to apologize if I said anything wrong, but she insisted that I hadn't. Instead, she thanked me for being thoughtful and after that, she just started opening up about all sorts of things. She told me about how she had met her husband as a teenager in church. He was her youth pastor and one day, he told her that God revealed it to him that she was going to be his wife. I guess the way it works in those circles is that once God reveals something to someone, with some sort of spiritual leadership, it's final. So, she obliged.

A few years later, they got married and that's when their child-bearing misfortunes started. It began with a couple miscarriages but then, when the third one happened, their gynecologist told them it wasn't going to be possible for her ever give birth. Again, I can't remember the medical reason for it. Anyway, according to her, that was when her husband changed. He became an angry person after that. He would get mad at the smallest things, and she somehow learnt how to manage the situation and you know, try to make him happy.

"I blame myself for making him that way," she said to me.

I asked her why.

She answered, "He's frustrated by our plight, but he lashes out on everything around him. He's a good man in a bad situation. If I could give him a child, maybe he wouldn't be this way."

She was making excuses for him; can you believe that? I don't know but that seemed crazy to me – and

I told her that.

She replied, "We are all victims of our circumstances. There are different sides to each of us and depending on the situation we find ourselves in, we could be one thing today and be another tomorrow. Think of it like a Rubik's cube. Every time you throw a Rubik's cube on the ground, a different side with a different color would be on top. Yet, it's the same Rubik's cube. That's how humans are. All I'm saying is, put him in a different situation and he could be a different man – a much better one."

Then, she hugged me and apologized on his behalf. No one ever held me like that. I could sense how genuine she was. I could tell that she truly wished me well and wasn't happy about everything that had been going on. This woman was as pure as the driven snow, I tell you.

I thanked her and before she left my room, that afternoon, she said, "One day, you too might find yourself in situations beyond your control. When that happens, do your best to be true to yourself. Have one color on all sides."

Damn, now that I think of it, that's really deep. Don't you think so?

What? Did I listen to her? I don't know.

I don't know if I've dealt with different situations in my life in the best way possible. You know, sometimes you don't know life is testing you until you come out on the other side, but you live and learn, you know what I mean?

No one ever said those words to me. Not in that way.

Anyway, the next morning, her husband called the social workers himself and he kicked us out. I cried that day. I was so pissed off, you know why? I thought this might be an opportunity for me actually fill the void of a guardian with the warmth of a stranger. In some ways, as bittersweet as it felt at the time, it was the best thing that happened to Ade and me. We moved in with another foster family in the city and things got a bit better for us. Today, we are good. We've got some cash – and sometimes, I send her money.

No, not my sister, the woman with the crazy husband. I send her money, sometimes.

What does it matter if I told you her name? You wouldn't know her. What is this? An interrogation?

One more question? Sure, shoot but this is the last one. I'm tired of talking.

A party? When? In college? I went to all sorts of parties in college, you have to be more specific.

Yeah, I think I remember that. Freshman year, it was a Halloween party. Yeah, I remember that. That was one of my craziest night in college. It was a …

Who? I danced with who?

I did what?

You don't know what you're talking about.

Wait a minute, who the hell are you?

PART THREE

NINE

May 19, 2017

She was doing a 140 on Route 90.

Kim had to. She had been delayed by a cop a few minutes ago and now, she was losing her tail on Chris' car. The evening hadn't gone exactly as planned but she was going to improvise her way through the rest of it. All she wanted to do was have a conversation with Chris, but it was beginning to look like she would have to do a little more than that.

"Goddamnit!" She slammed her palms on the steering wheels.

Chris' car was out of sight at this point. Underneath her breath, she cursed the cop who had pulled her over earlier for speeding. Again, she had pulled a sad story card on this cop and again, she was able to get away scot-free but this time, the cop decided to share some unwarranted words of wisdom with her before he let her go.

"Be careful on the road." The cop said after deciding not to issue her a fine, "There's a section of Route 90 where the streetlights don't work so be careful out there. Don't go speeding, you could end up in a ditch."

"Thank you, I won't." She shot a glance at the name tag that sat above his shirt pocket, "Thank you, officer Ludric."

"You're welcome," He stepped away from the car.

As she was about to wind up the car window, the officer moved back into the frame and peered through the window.

"Whatever you're chasing, let it go." He spoke in hoarse whispers, "The longer we hold onto things, the more we lose sight of what's ahead."

"What?" Kim was stunned by his sudden rhetoric, "What are you talking about?"

"I'm just saying," He shrugged, "Take a page off Jesus' book: to forgive is to heal. Have a great day, ma'am."

With that, the officer strode back to his car which was parked behind hers. Through the wing mirror on the driver's side of her car, her eyes followed the officer as he got into his car and sped away.

Now, as she continued her chase, she couldn't get those words out of her head.

To forgive is to heal.

"Who does he think he is?" Kim thought to herself, *"The nerves on him!"*

She looked over at the GPS that sat above the automotive head unit of her car. According to the GPS, she was about 30 minutes away from Rochester. By her calculations, Chris was probably 10 minutes ahead of her. If she was going to catch him, she would have to keep driving at about 140 km/h.

As she drove past 14th street, which spread right into Mapleview, she caught sight of a license plate off the highway but just ahead of her. It was Chris'. The car was parked in a lot and there was a motel sign right in front of it. Unable to quickly bring the car to a halt, she sped past Chris' car and kept driving until she found a suitable spot to make a complete U-turn. She parked her car right beside Chris' and looked over to see if there was anyone in his car. It was empty. Immediately, she jumped right out and began kicking at the trunk, hoping to get it unlocked, somehow.

Kim's mind was racing: Earlier, she had seen Chris knock Beth out, throw her body into the trunk and then drive away. From where she had been seating, in her parked car in the parking lot at the garden, she had filmed the whole thing but when she realized how fast their argument had escalated, she knew she had to do something so she sped after Chris, trying to keep a safe distance from his car.

Now, all she wanted to do was find a way to help Beth. She had thought about calling the cops and even considered talking to officer Ludric about it earlier, but she still wanted to have a one-on-one conversation with Chris and if she called the cops too soon, she wouldn't get the chance to speak with him privately.

The trunk wasn't opening, and all Kim's kicking was for naught. She walked away from the car and strode into the motel. The motel door opened into a reception room and to the left of the room was a door that led into a bar. A grey-haired man with a pair of glasses hanging over his nose stood on the other end of the counter in the reception.

"Hello," The grey-haired man greeted her, "Welcome to Maple Motel. How can I help you?"

"Hi, I'm looking for…" Kim stepped up to the counter but before she could complete her sentence or stride, she saw him from the corner of her eyes, through the door that led into the bar. It was Chris. He was sitting at the bar with a bottle of beer in one hand.

"What are you looking for, ma'am?" The grey-haired man called her attention back to him.

"Oh, uhm, just the bar. I'm looking for the bar." She replied, "but I see it's just right there."

"Yeah, right through that door."

"Sure, thank you."

With that, Kim walked into the bar. She cast her eyes around the hostelry – there were tables and barstools laid out across the room and the wall was decorated with neon signages on all sides. Other than Chris, two other people were in there. The bartender who stood across the bar counter from Chris and man in a baseball cap, seated at the far corner of the room, peering out through the window.

Chris was right there - about six feet from her. Her mind flashed back to the night of the Halloween party. The memories were vivid. She remembered how she had pleaded with him to stop and how it seemed like the more she begged, the more forceful he got. She never thought she would ever have to meet him again and if she ever did, she had been certain she wouldn't be able to bear it. Yet, here she was – in the same room with the man who violated her youth, created the ripple effect that worsened her medical condition and banished her to a life without an offspring. This is the climax of it all. The moment she has dreaded for a long time.

Kim's train of thought was suddenly halted by Chris' movement. She was still making her way towards one of the barstools in front of the bar table when he stood up, dropped two bills on the bar table, nodded at the bartender and walked right past her out of the bar. Everything within her froze as he walked past her. For a second, she shut her eye and tried to catch her breath. One of her biggest fears about this moment was that he might actually recognize her and act out as a result but instead he had walked right past her. Clearly, he didn't know who she was.

She let a few seconds pass before she turned around and walked out of the bar, back into the reception. Chris wasn't there.

"Hi," She gestured at the grey-haired man, "did you see a black guy walk out of the bar just now?"

"Yeah," the grey-haired man replied, "He's right outside on the balcony, taking a puff at his cigarette."

"Oh, thank you."

She exited the reception and there he was, again, doing exactly as the grey-haired receptionist had suggested. Chris stood, bent over the railing of the balcony, with a cigarette in his right hand. Kim took a deep and long breath, summoned all the courage within her and walked up to him.

"Hi." She started and waited for him to turn towards her before she continued, "how's it going?"

"Good, good." He replied and took a dekko at her from head to toe as if he were sizing her up.

"Do you think I could burn a smoke off you?" She asked, hoping to God that he had an extra cigarette on him.

"Sure."

Much to her delight, Kim watched as Chris reached into the pocket on the right side of his pants, brought out a pack of cigarette and extended it towards her. After she had pulled a stick out of the pack, he pulled out a lighter and held it in her direction to help her light up her stick.

"Thank you." She said as she took a drag on the cigarette in her hand, "Lovely weather today, don't you think?"

"Hmmm." Chris nodded.

"Forecast said it was going to rain but it's good to see that weather gods had mercy on us today."

"Yeah, I guess." He tilted his head from side to side as a gesture to affirm her statement.

He wasn't being much a talker so Kim knew she would her to make somewhat of an extra effort to get him to speak with her.

"Are you from around here?" She asked.

"Uhm, no." He answered, "Just visiting. How about you?"

"Just visiting too, actually." She was glad he was responsive enough to throw the question back at her, "Came out here to meet someone but I'll be heading right back home in the morning."

"Where's home?"

"Canada."

"Really?" His eyes lit up at her response, "I live there as well. Whereabout are you from exactly?"

"Winnipeg."

"No way! That's where I'm from as well. That's cool. I'm Christian, by the way."

He extended his arm to give her a handshake.

"Kimberly," She shook his hand, "Nice to meet

you."

"Nice to meet you too. Did you get to meet the person you came out here to see?"

Realizing the irony in Chris' question, Kim grinned from ear to ear. She wasn't sure how to play this, but she knew what she wanted the end result to look like. For now, she had resolved to go with the flow of things and seeing where their conversation would lead them. Yet, as she went along with the flow, she couldn't get Beth out of her mind. Kim wondered if she was still alive and regardless of if she was alive or not, what had he done with her.

"Yes, I have met the person. I think it was worthwhile making the trip down here. I needed it."

"Yeah? That's good. I wish I could say the same but I'm beginning to regret coming out here."

"Regret, eh?" She shot a glance at him, doing her best to act clueless, "How come? Everything okay?"

"Yeah, for the most part." He replied, "Just hit a bump in the road. It's under control though. Nothing I can't handle; you know what I mean?"

"It happens, I guess." She nodded, "How long are you out here for?"

"I was supposed to be out here till Sunday but right now, I'm not so sure. I might have to get back to the city earlier than I planned."

"Oh, your bump in the road is that bad, yeah?"

"Yeah, yeah. I'll fix it though."

"Sorry about that."

"You smoke weed?" Chris asked.

Kim was amazed by how he had casually asked the question, given the fact that they were across the border and in a country where such vices weren't tolerated. Yet, she went with the flow.

"Uhm, who's asking?"

Her reply triggered a peal of laughter out of Chris.

"Don't worry, I'm not a cop."

"That's exactly what an undercover cop would say, don't you think so?"

"True, but I'm not." He said, mid-laughter, "I just need someone to smoke with."

"Sure." Kim raised her shoulders up slightly and then dropped them.

"I've got some rolled up upstairs."

"Upstairs?"

"Yeah, I'm lodged here," Chris replied, "Right upstairs. Room 104."

"Are you going to go get it or?" Kim asked, hoping he wouldn't invite her upstairs to his room. The last thing she wanted was to be in a room with him. Then again, she didn't want to kill the vibe they had going on by rejecting his advances.

"Yeah, yeah." Chris started making his way towards the stairs at the end of the balcony, "I'll be right back."

While Chris was momentarily away from her, Kim pulled out her iPhone from her pocket. The time on the home screen read 12:09 am. The night was far spent but she was keen on making the most of it. She placed her right thumb on the home button to unlock the phone and then, she tapped her Safari app. Once the browser opened up, she googled the number of the local Rochester police department and saved it as a speed dial. Then, she opened up her Voice Memo app and tapped the red button. Her plan was to record their conversation in case Chris confessed or admitted what he did to her and now, Beth.

As she waited for Chris to return from his room, Kim considered all she had had to do to get here from finally opening up about everything to her husband to admitting that she needed to speak with Chris before she could really move on, to tracking him down, and then working with Amina to trail him all the way to Minnesota. It hadn't all worked out the way she thought it would, but something was in play here and she was willing to see it through.

"Alright, I think we are good to go." Chris emerged from the staircase, "One more issue though."

Kim quickly put her phone away as he appeared. She could tell that he was enjoying her company, so she feigned a response by squealing with delight.

"Woohoo! Whatever could this issue be?"

"We are in Minnesota." Chris said, "This stuff isn't legal here. We have to find a place to smoke it where no one can see us."

"Good point!" She placed a finger over her lips then looked up, as if she was deep in thought, "I think I've got an idea, Christian."

"What are you thinking, Kimberly?"

"My car. It's right there. We could smoke in there and keep talking. No one's going to know."

"You sure, I mean, it's right there in the parking lot. Anyone could still see us."

"I think we are overthinking this, Christian." Kim shrugged, "We are in Rochester, Minnesota. There's no weed-seeking-police division out here. No one's going to know. We could smoke in the car, so no one has to deal with the tang from it."

"Sure, let's do it!"

Together, they walked out from the balcony to the parking lot and strolled to Kim's car – which was parked next to Chris'. Although, Kim acted like she didn't know the car was his. As they walked, with Chris just a foot ahead of her, she took a good look at him. To an extent, she could see how Chris could easily come across as someone with a genteel upbringing. She wondered how someone so decent looking, successful and seemingly well-mannered be so dangerous.

As they arrived at her car, Chris stood beside her as though he was about to go through the door behind the driver's seat, but she motioned at him to get into front passenger seat instead while she sat in the driver's seat.

"Are we actually driving anywhere? Or we are just going to be parked out here?" He asked as he shut the door to the front passenger seat.

"No, I don't think we have to." She replied, "We can just sit here and talk."

"Fine by me."

"You're married, eh?" Kim gestured towards the ring on the fourth finger on Chris' right hand.

"Uhm," Chris shot a glance at the ring, "Yeah, I am. Not for long though."

"Oh, trouble in paradise?"

"It was barely ever paradise." Chris raised his eyebrows, "At least, not for me."

"So, you're getting a divorce? Or what's going on there?"

"Yeah, I plan to. When I get back to the city, you know what I mean."

"Tell me about her." Kim repositioned herself in the driver seat so she could look directly at him.

"Who?"

"Your wife, tell me about her."

"I don't want to talk about her." Chris shook his head in disagreement, "Come on, don't make me do that. We are here, she's not. What does it matter? You know what I mean?"

"How did you meet her?" Kim asked,

"What? What was that?"

"How did you meet her?"

"How did I meet her? Come on, why does it matter? Okay, you know what? If I tell you, would you let this go? Cause, to be honest, I don't think we need to go into all those details. Clearly, you're cool with this so everything else shouldn't matter, you know what I mean?"

"Yeah, we are just talking." Kim said, "That's all."

"Sure, sure." Chris nodded his head, lit up one of the rolled papers he had picked up from his room, took a whiff of it then passed it on to Kim.

TEN

May 20, 2017

"Wait a minute, who the hell are you?" Chris barked at her.

Startled, Kim moved back a bit and got closer to the car door than she was to the gear stick in between them. She could see the vein in his neck pop. The seemingly well-mannered man who had been telling her interesting stories about his childhood was morphing into an angry and ferocious beast. She had to use her knowledge of psychology to tame him.

"Christian, you don't need to get…"

"Don't call me that!" He snapped, "Who are you?"

"Listen," Kim tried to speak as softly as she could, "I'm not trying to get you all riled up. We are just talking but I need you to know something."

"Who are you?" Chris repeated, "Why are you talking to me right now?"

It was at this point that Kim realized that Chris wasn't angry. He was actually scared and whenever he got scared, he resorted to violence of some sort. That was why he had attacked Beth when she wouldn't stop calling him a rapist. With this in mind, Kim approached the situation differently.

"You don't have to be scared. I'm not going to do anything to you. I am not accusing you of something you didn't do. I'm simply reminding you of something you did."

Kim paused, sighed and then said, "something you did to me."

That calmed him down. He just stared at her and remained speechless.

"Yes, Christian." Kim continued, "I know about that Halloween party because I was there. We were both there and you raped me that night."

Chris began shaking his head slowly, and in belief, "No, no, no. You're making this up. You're trying to set me up."

"I'm not. You know what I am talking about. There's no need to act like we both don't know. I'm not going to do anything to you. I just want to talk to you about it so I can move on."

He went mute after she said that and then after a short while, he looked up at her. His eyes were bloodshot red as he said, "I remember that night."

"Okay, that's a step." Kim said, "Do you remember what happened that night?"

Chris ignored her question, looked and simply said, "I'm sorry. I shouldn't have done that to you."

Kim was relieved that he actually admitted it. She

was making progress and she knew it.

"Yes, Christian, you shouldn't." Kim said, "What you did that night hurt me deeply. It shattered everything I thought I knew about myself and life, as a whole. I lost a lot of blood that night and I almost died. Even after I survived it, for months long after it happened, I contemplated committing suicide. I didn't think I could ever have sex again. In fact, anything that had to with sex irked me for a while. All because of that one night. So, yes. Yes, Christian, you shouldn't have done that."

"I know that." Chris said, "I mean, in hindsight, I know that. I don't know what came over me but that night, we just started going at it and at some point, I just couldn't control myself."

"You can always control yourself, Christian. When another human is screaming at you and telling you no, your mind registers that and your body can choose to follow suit. You can and could've controlled yourself. I live with a medical condition, today, that may have been triggered by what you did that night."

"What's that?" Chris put his palms together and raise them to his jaw as he listened intently to Kim.

"Endometriosis. It's a long story and I can't go into that, but I just want you to know that your actions that night had grievous impact on my life."

"I was wrong," Chris said, "I was wrong and I'm sorry."

"Are you though?" Kim could feel her eyes get teary as she spoke, but she managed to keep herself together. "I don't quite believe you are."

"I am. Swear to God, I am."

"If you are, why do you do the same to your wife?" Kim did her best to continue speaking as softly as she could, "Why did you do what you just did to your girlfriend, Beth? Why do you take the females in your life for granted? Is Beth even alive? What have you done with her?"

"Oh, God." Chris wrapped his head with hands, "You know about Beth? How do you know about this? Have you been tailing me or something? Did you call the cops on me? Are they waiting for some signal from you?"

The fear was back.

Kim noticed how Chris was palpitating with terror. It didn't take long for him to break down and start crying. That took Kim by surprise. She hadn't expected him to admit to anything talk less of actually crying over it, but she didn't come all this way to watch a rapist cry.

"No," She spoke sternly, "Christian, listen to me! You don't get to cry and act like a victim. So, wipe those tears and let's talk."

"I'm not acting like a victim," Chris muttered, "I'm genuinely sorry."

"If you are, then tell me where's Beth? Where is she?"

"She's upstairs in my room."

"Dead or alive?" Kim asked,

"She's alive but she's knocked out cold and could wake up anytime now, but I don't know what to do when she wakes up. I really love her, and I made a mistake when I laid my…"

"That's enough, Christian." Kim cut in, "Can I have your room keys, please?"

"Why?"

"I'm going to help you take care of your mess with Beth."

Chris unwrapped his head from his hands and shot a puzzled look at her.

"What does that mean?" He asked,

"I'm going to help you take care of Beth."

"Why would you do that?"

"Because we are going to have a deal right now and you are going to do exactly as I say." Kim said, "I have a video recording of you and Beth today in the parking lot and I can always hand it over to the cops. Also, I have been recording our conversation all this time – including just now when you admitted that you raped me and your wife and that you hit Beth. That plus some of the other outrageous things you've said in the past hour. I can use all these against you, but I won't. Instead, you will do as I say."

"What do you want? Money?"

Kim smirked, "I don't need your money but here's what I need you to do. I'm going to give you my card and you will contact me when you are back in the city. I'm a psychotherapist so I'm going to take you on as one of my patients. Contact me when you are back in the city and we will schedule sessions together. The second thing I need you to do is to go back to the city as soon as you can. Go there and be with your wife. Forget about Beth."

"No, I can't do that." Chris shook his head, slowly, like a hurt puppy.

"What can't you do?"

"I can't leave Beth. I can't lose her."

"Are you daft, Christian?" Kim pursed her mouth and leered at him, "The minute you hit her, you already lost her, but you know what you still have? A wife and you are going to go home and do your best to be a good husband to her. I will help Beth recover, I won't tell the cops, and you will report to me for therapy sessions otherwise I will send everything I have on you to the police. Believe me, I have more than just this. I hired a private investigator to trail you for months. I know all about some of the shady investments you've made – especially with your new app, Ponyr. I don't care about any of that, but I will use the information I have if I have to. But Christian, don't make me do that."

"This is crazy." Chris muttered, "You did all that just to get me to come to therapy sessions?"

"I would advise you to say fewer words from now on. I did all that so I can have you by the balls. I did all that so I could know more about the man who hurt me. If I didn't do what I did, I wouldn't have been able to, anonymously, send information to Beth about how you've raped your wife multiple times in the past couple years. If my friend, Amina, your jeweler, hadn't given me heads up about your plans with Beth, I wouldn't have been here to catch you slamming her head against a car. Only God knows what you would have done with the poor girl."

"I wouldn't have done anything to her. I swear I panicked when I put her in my trunk. I didn't know what to do." Chris said, "I was on my way to the hospital but then she woke up, and so…"

"Shut the hell up, Christian!" Even Kim didn't know when she began screaming, yet she continued, "You threw her in a trunk. You can't claim to love someone and then, knowingly, hurt them. That's not how love works. You are a freaking clueless idiot."

Chris went mute and listened as Kim went on a tirade of rebukes. When she was done, he asked her one more question, "So, why are you helping me? Why aren't you calling the cops right now?"

"I was going to call the cops." Kim replied, "But I heard your story and I know that one of the reasons you are acting the way you've done all these years is because you had a traumatic and abusive childhood. You lost your parents at a young age. You were neglected by your parents and sexually assaulted by your aunt. You were also physically, emotionally and verbally abused, multiple times; and most of all, you never dealt with any of these things so whether you know it or not, you are experiencing a posttraumatic stress disorder – and it is manifesting itself through your acts of sexual violence and fits of rage.

"Just look at what you did to Beth. I hope to God that she is alive like you said she is, but the fact is you could have killed her. You were this close to committing homicide. When you hurt me, years ago, you were also this close to committing sexual homicide. There is a pattern here and a seasoned researcher, by the name – Ann Burgess – coined a theory about this. Everything about your upbringing – from your social environment to those key formative events of your life to the way you were patterned to respond to these events and to others and then down to how you were treated by those you hold dear to you – everything has had an impact on your life. According to Ann Burgess, these psychosocial and cognitive factors make you a potential perpetrator of sexual homicide.

"I'm willing to work with you to identify these factors, deal with them one by one and help you regain a better sense of self but first, go home to your wife and be good to her."

EPILOGUE

May 22, 2017

The smell of manure filled the air, announcing the arrival of the slurry spreading season. Unfortunately, this earthly redolence was not enough to simmer down the hustle and bustle of the rush hour.

Car honks blared as impatient and weary drivers navigated their way through the 5 pm traffic to their homes. One by one, they wheeled towards the comforts of a place that had nothing in common with school or work. The stench was the last thing on their minds. It was as though the promise of their final destinations had softened their olfactory senses.

Alicia could sense it all - the funk, noise and restlessness. She knew this city, its culture and people too well. Everything and everyone in this city always seem to be on a biblical exodus; moving towards a destination of promise but consumed by wanderlust. She knew better. She didn't buy into the culture.

"There is no such thing as a destination of promise." Alicia once said to Francis, her therapist, "That's a fantasy that keeps people from being in the moment. I don't believe in all that, you know, not being in the moment."

"What if the moment's too much to take in?" Francis shot back.

"Take what you get, the moment is the moment for a reason." said Alicia, "We keep waiting for something better, you know. We tell ourselves the best is yet to come. What if it never gets better? What if your best has passed? It's a dangerous thing to do, you know."

"What is? What's dangerous?"

"Hope." Alicia took a gulp from the glass of water he had just offered her "It's dangerous to put all your eggs in some futuristic basket."

"For many people, hope is all they have. Sometimes, even in the moment, hope is all you get; and as you said, you have to take what you get."

Alicia wouldn't budge. She was a realist - the kind who didn't believe in other realms of idealism or in those who held them. She believed that life moves in one direction, forward; and so, should we.

She gently stepped on her brakes to give room for a Honda Civic, whose driver was trying to turn into her lane. The traffic wasn't getting any better, but she was still on time. Chris wouldn't be home for another two hours, that should give her enough time to weave through the traffic, get home and make his favorite dish - pounded yam and egusi soup.

She had no idea why he loved pounded yam and

egusi soup so much, but he did anyway. Three years ago, while they were still dating, Alicia decided to learn how to cook it. That Christmas, Chris' twin sister, Ade, had flown into town to see him. Ade rang up Alicia's phone on the morning of Christmas Eve and suggested they both went grocery shopping to prepare for the festivities that would begin the next day and run all the way into the new year.

Although they had only met six months prior, Ade was fond of Alicia and spent more time on the phone with her than with her twin.

"Don't you know the way to a man's heart is through his stomach?" Ade said, with a grin, as the girls walked down Aisle 12 - the international foods aisle - of the store.

Alicia laughed; she was used to Ade's silly jokes but wanted to know where this one was going.

"I already have my man's heart and food has nothing to do with it," Alicia said,

"Trust me, girl, I know my brother. He loves food."

"Yeah, sure I know that too." Alicia's face turned stern for a second. "Wait, did he complain to you about me or my cooking or something?"

"No." Ade ran her fingers across her long dark hair and moved it out of the way as she stooped low, to grab two packs of shortbread from the bottom rack of the shelf. "No, he didn't. It's just… you know what his favorite food is right?"

"The yam and soup thing?"

"Yeah, pounded yam. He loves that. Back home, if you want to get your man to do something for you, you whip up some nice meal that he can't resist and then you are game."

Alicia burst out laughing, "Sounds like a lot of stress

though, why not just ask?"

If there is anything Alicia had learned about Chris' culture, it was its intensity. Everything is really everything over there. Emotions are heightened, families are extended, relationships are never casual, and pronunciations are stretched. She would joke with Chris about how he had no sense of moderation, but she knew where he got that from.

"Penny for your thoughts, take it or leave it." Ade was in big sister mode now, "I don't want you to ever feel... you know, culture shock or something."

"What do you mean?"

"I'm sure there are so many cultural differences between you two that you're probably still trying to learn and understand. I never want them to overwhelm you. So, if you have any questions or you know, for clarity's sake or something, I'm always a phone call away."

Alicia believed her. Ade had been supportive and kind to her ever since they met. Ade - and her twin - were just two years older than she was but for Ade, that was enough age gap to claim the title and responsibility of being Alicia's big sister whenever she felt the need to; and this was one of those moments.

"Thanks, Ade." Alicia dropped some of the grocery items on the cashier's carousel. "I'm sure I'll be fine, but I might take you up on that offer sometime."

That evening, Ade taught Alicia how to cook pounded yam. She had begun by warning Alicia the method they were using wasn't the original way of cooking it. The right way would be to cut a tuber of yam into small bits, boil them and use a pestle to grind them in a mortar. Over here in Canada, that wasn't a realistic possibility - no one sold yam tubers around here - so instead, Ade simply boiled and swirled yam flour to make pounded yam. Alicia preferred the latter method.

After spending a few months, watching videos on YouTube, reading some articles online and making a mess in her kitchen, Alicia cooked up a storm of pounded yam and egusi soup on one of her and Chris' date nights. Since then, it has been her go-to surprise dish for Chris.

Today's dinner was going to feature that surprise dish. Chris had spent the past couple of weeks on a business trip and was going to be back home in a couple of hours. To welcome him, Alicia had originally planned a night out in town for both of them, but the weather forecast had messed up those plans. She had no choice but to change the plan and resort to her go-to surprise dish.

The stench was beginning to subside as she pulled into her driveway. About a year ago, right after getting married, she and Chris moved into this neighborhood. It was one of the city's more affluent neighborhoods. Granted, it was a bargain as the only price its resident had to pay for earning a good income and being able to afford homes in this area was the serenity and absolute quiet that came with it. Living here was as good as living in the outskirts of the city.

Alicia didn't mind it. Chris had made a good fortune for himself to be able to afford such a space and she was proud of him for that. Despite the fact that all the wives she had met here were at least twice as old as she was, she liked it here. Once in a while, she would wander around the nabe and bask in its tranquility and beauty.

Right now, these perks were not peculiar enough

for Alicia to ignore the stench that was in the air. She wanted nothing more than to get into the house, safe and away from the funk. She had taken in more whiffs of aerated manure than one should bear; she parked the car, grabbed her bag, made her way to the front door but stopped mid-stride.

The front door was wide open. Stunned, she retraced her steps back to earlier in the day - in the morning - trying to remember whether or not she had actually locked the door on her way to work. Every morning was a routine and a regular part of that routine was locking her front door. Regardless of how safe and tranquil this neighborhood may be, no one would want to throw caution to the wind by not closing or locking their doors. Especially Alicia, she wouldn't. She was as cautious as a fox - everyone who knew her knew that. She loved her space but, more importantly, she loved keeping her space safe.

Chris. He was the first thing that came to mind.

Maybe he got back home earlier than planned and left the door open? Or is he playing some kind of joke on me?

She took a gander around her to be sure his car wasn't anywhere in sight or someone wasn't watching. It wasn't and no one was. She shrugged her wandering thoughts off and walked in anyway. Closing and locking the door behind her, she took a quick glance around the parlor that spread across the main floor and led to the kitchen and stairway. Everything seemed to be in place.

The rich-reddish brown wood that separated the basement from the first floor looked as shiny as she had left it. None of the wall frames or paintings were out of place - not even by an inch. Nothing was out of place. Everything seemed to be in place.

What are you up to, Chris?

Within a few seconds, her eyes scanned the expanse of the room and she made her way to the kitchen on the far end of the room. The kitchen, with its Tuscan-style interior design, had a traditional vibe like it has been lived in or used for centuries. The terracotta-colored cabinetry and the translucent curtains had a certain poise to it, one that was synonymous with both the relaxed tradition of Tuscany and Alicia's serene neighborhood.

It was everything she wanted in a kitchen, everything she had planned it to be - and right now it looked as intact as she had left it this morning. As she stood staring at the luxurious kitchen, the side of her eye caught a knife on the table. She moved closer to have a better look - there was a red smear on it. She recognized the smear but didn't want to believe it. It was blood.

At that moment, she saw the rest of it. Right beside the countertop, a pool of blood covered a significant area of the kitchen floor. There was no smell or footprints or anything, just blood.

Alicia didn't move. Her heart raced but she tried her best to stay calm. She wanted to scream or run but restrained herself. She was scared she would make a sound and whatever or whoever else may be in the house would hear her and come after her. She stood still.

She dipped her left hand in her handbag, trying to reach for her phone.

911, I should call 911.

But it didn't make sense. There was no sign of blood anywhere else. The rest of the first floor looked impeccable except for the knife on the countertop and the small pool of blood. Whatever may have happened, there ought to be more signs or pointers, more disruptions. Everything shouldn't be in placc.

She pressed her thumb on her phone's center button to unlock it, opened her phone app and speed dialed Chris. He had to know, first. Someone had broken into their home and smeared blood in their kitchen. Whatever the case may be, he had to know what was going on. If anything happens, from here on out, he shouldn't have to hear it from the news or cops.

Placing the phone against her ear, she glanced at the digital timer on the electric stove that was attached to the kitchen wall. 5:45pm. Chris' plane should still be in the air by now, his phone would be on airplane mode. Yet, the phone rang and from where she stood, she could hear the ringtone.

She wasn't imagining things. An iPhone's marimba ringtone was blaring, and she could hear it. It was coming from upstairs - right above her, the master bedroom. Chris' phone was ringing from the bedroom. She stopped the call, redialed it and the ringtone went blaring again.

"Chris!" She shouted, making her way for the staircase at the other corner of the room. "Chris, are you home?"

The stillness was gone, now she was really panicking. She ran up the stairs to the second floor, moving towards the direction of the ringtone. On the wall, between the top of the stairs and master bedroom were three framed pictures.

From the corner of her eye, she caught a quick glance at the painting in the middle. It was a picture of their wedding day. Ade had just finished giving her speech at the reception ceremony. Her words had left Chris and Alicia blushing, and, in that instance, the camera's lights flashed and captured the moment - with the newly wedded couple grinning from ear to ear. It had made for a beautiful picture and brought back memories.

Memories, moments, pictures - they could end up being all she has. Francis was wrong. The past was past, and the present is really all she can hold on to. Anything could happen any moment and that ship called hope could be upended. Despite all that had happened between them, Alicia cherished the memories she had made with Chris - good and bad - but she had to be realistic about the future. Whatever was happening right now could change everything. She could lose everything but that picture on the wall was a reminder of memories she still had.

Chris had the picture framed and hung on the wall shortly after the wedding. She noticed the smiles weren't there anymore. Their faces had been carelessly torn from the picture leaving the frame dangling from the nail that held it to the wall.

More signs.

At this point, she was convinced this was an attack or some kind of raid. Anything or anyone could be behind the master bedroom's door. She knew she ought to be running in the opposite direction or calling 911 but that made less sense. What if Chris was in there? She had to be sure. She had to face her future head-on.

The ringtone was still blaring from inside the room as she pushed against the door. It was locked.

"Chris!" She screamed,

Forcing her weight on the door, she picked out a key from a bunch and entered it into the keyhole, twisting it until it opened. When the door finally opened, she saw it. She knew what it meant. It was like a million and one thoughts were going through her mind but, at the same time, she couldn't think. She could see her whole life - or at least the one she had had with Chris - flash before her eyes.

He was gone. Chris laid lifeless on their matrimonial bed. She rushed at him, shaking him and sobbing loudly. He was dead, she knew it as soon as she saw him. No one else was in the room. He just laid there, on the bed, covered with stab marks and in a pool of blood.

With all the energy she could muster, she shook him, as if her swaying could somehow bring him back to life or wake her up from this nightmare. She could feel herself unwinding, her thoughts wandering, future dimming, and lights shutting off. Everything was not in place, not anymore.

No movie she's watched or story she had heard or read about a wife finding her husband dead could have described this moment. This was it; this is real. Chris is dead.

Half an hour went by before she grabbed her phone and dialed 911. An operator picked up the call.

"I have an emergency." Alicia spoke into the phone, gasping, "He's gone. My husband's gone."

Tobi Nifesi

The Burgess Theory

Special thanks to:
AyoOluwa Akinduro
Chidera Ogueri
Christiana Okonko
Damm-e Olasehinde
Desiree Obafisoye
Elizabeth Olojede
Esther Olatunji
Funmilola Ogunseye
Gloria Thompson
Jane Frances Ekwueme
Juanita Aganbi
Kaosisochukwu Nzeagwu
Kerhaamor
Michael Imoru
Mwila Mvula
Oghenekefe Aomreore
Olivia Onuk
Omoayo Bakare
Oyinda Alaka
Oyindamola Olanrewaju
Oyinkansola Bolaji-Idowu
Oyinkansola Oluwaji
Orobosa Ikponmwen
Pherkeh
Precious Ibrah
Rit Piwuna
Rose Elekanachi
Sandra Imagbe
Theresa Simba
Toluwalope Dare
Tope Olunifesi
Vanessa Aganbi
Wole Jr

Sexual assault is any type of sexual activity or contact that you do not consent to. Sexual assault can happen through physical force or threats of force or if the attacker gave the victim drugs or alcohol as part of the assault. Sexual assault includes rape and sexual coercion. (Office on Women's Health)

Visit tobinifesi.com/sexualassault to learn more about Sexual Assault.

Report incidents of sexual assault by calling your city's sexual assault hotline or 911.

ABOUT TOBI NIFESI

Tobi Nifesi is a writer who harnesses the intrusive power of the pen as a tool to pave a path that opens up to enlightenment and redemption. He believes that by writing he can create, recreate and share stories that are just as intriguing as they are awakening.

He is the cofounder of horoma - a creative storytelling and content strategy platform - and a journalist who has worked with publications such as Maclean's Magazine, the Manitoban Newspaper and Interlake Spectator.

Tobi believes in Linkin' Park, 'Mad Men' television series, Dan Brown, Apple and Jesus.

www.ingramcontent.com/pod-product-compliance
Lightning Source LLC
Chambersburg PA
CBHW052006220626
47052CB00004B/1116